Pana-Mania

By
C. M. Schrecengost

ISBN (Paperback): 978-1-7377512-0-5
ISBN (EBook): 978-1-7377512-1-2
Library of Congress Control Number: 2021916232
Any reference to historical events, real people, or real
places are used fictitiously. Names, characters, and places are
products of the Author's imagination.
Front cover image by Artist.
Book design by Designer.
First print edition 2021.
Published in Swansboro, NC

Pana-Mania

Contents

Acknowledgments

To my loving family, whom supported me throughout the perilous journey of writing, and publication.

Introduction

The nauseating aroma of alcohol oozes forth from every pore in Decker Costley's body as withdrawal begins to set in, and perspiration on his lip increases. Stumbling from alleyway to alleyway with the loud scraping of his shoes, he says through wheezing breaths, "Imani! Where are you, baby?!"

Fumbling around every dark corner of Manhattan, he clutches to his jacket as the cold night saturates his bones. A loud and aggressive cough rattles his mucus filled lungs, and he struggles to catch his breath.

"Lord, help me find my baby. I swear I won't ever ask you for another thing. Please, please just return Imani to us."

Slumping to the ground and tirelessly sobbing, he places his hands to his head and begins to rock back and forth against an old brick wall of a nearby building. Pulling at the long and frizzy unmaintained hair upon his head, he growls and begins to hit himself while saying, "Stupid, stupid, stupid, he's not going to help you. Never does, and never will."

Looking up to the sky, he shouts, "All those years of devotion, and nothing? Fine! I don't need you anymore!"

He pushes himself from the cold pavement and staggers into the nearest alley. With blurred vision, he looks into the darkened area ahead and sees the silhouette of a young woman flash by. Out stretching his arm to wave, he calls with desperation in his voice, "Imani! It's me baby! Daddy's here!"

The shadow figure reappears further away and Decker squints his eyes, trying to focus.

"Wh-why are you running, baby? Come on home!"

Unable to make out any facial features, he steps forward. Moving in tandem, the silhouette also draws closer. Only about five yards out, Decker struggles to walk in a straight line, and stumbles into an older homeless man. "Watch where you're going!" The soiled old man shouts through brown gritted teeth. Still staring through a furrowed brow, he positions his hands over a nearby burn barrel, and shivers.

Decker slurs, "I'm-sorry," and turns his focus back to the silhouette. Progressing only a couple of paces without pause, Decker and the figure stand within feet of each other. Through chattering teeth, he says, "Why are you hiding? We've missed you so much."

Receiving no answer, Decker thoughtlessly beckons for a hug with outstretched arms and palms wide open. Just then, the figure steps out of the shadows. Now looking upon a man dressed in all black, wearing a mask and hoodie, he mumbles, "You're not Imani."

The man ominously tilts his head to the side and says, "No, no I'm not," and pulls a chrome, six shot, snub-nosed revolver from his pocket.

"Say hello to Imani for me."

Widening his eyes, Decker says, "C-" before being shot in the chest at point-blank range.

Blood splatters the ground behind him and Decker falls flat on his back. As the muzzle flash of the revolver singes the stubble upon his chin and the scent of gunpowder invades his nostrils, the world around Decker starts to blur. Memories of his children running through an open field of assorted flowers with laughter in their bellies, scrolls through his mind like a movie on fast forward.

With the man standing over him, Decker uses the last of his life force saying, "Imani, Jake," before letting out a long exhale.

Still staring with his head tilted, the man lets out a low chuckle before saying, "You were always weak."

Having completed his task, he pulls a pair of shears from his pocket and reaches down for Decker's left hand. Spreading his lifeless fingers, the man positions the sheers and with a few squeezes, cuts off Decker's pinky.

Looking at the severed finger, he says, "That'll do nicely."

The murderous man veiled in black turns to leave, and sees the old bum by the fire staring in silence from just a few feet away. The mysterious man effortlessly lifts his revolver once more and empties the last of his shots. Hitting the ground with a loud thud, the homeless man lay lifeless but an arms distance from Decker. A large pool of blood begins to surround the bodies and without another word, the man in black casually makes his way down the dark alley and disappears into the night.

Pana-Mania

First Impressions

Ear piercing sirens, obnoxious revving engines, and the never-ceasing chatter of people reverberate throughout the exhaust permeated air in Jake Costley's nostrils. Regardless, he continues to walk the busy New York City streets nearing his apartment on a bright early morning without care. Gazing down, with both hands buried deep in his black jacket pockets, he quickly makes his way down a thin, gray, and crumbling sidewalk rounding a sharp corner that leads to a tight alleyway. Glancing up towards a metal and rust mixed fire escape bolted to the side of his apartment building, he removes his hands from his pockets and jumps to grab the ladder. With hands gripping the bottom rung, he drops all his weight, and the old ladder extends with a loud screech, and he begins to climb. Slippery step after slippery step, Jake begins to feel sweat form on his brow as the anticipation of entering through his bedroom window draws near.

"I hope Mama is still sleeping. I'd hate for her to find out that I've been out all night, again."

Having reached his window located on the second floor of the apartment building, he crouches on the landing and lifts his head just high enough to peer through the small gap between his blackout curtains.

"Coast looks clear. I better get moving."

Using extreme caution, he pulls a small knife from his front pocket and wedges it under the old wooden window seal. Taking very little effort, the window breaks free, and every so softly, he makes his way through it. Within seconds Jake closes the window and creeps to the other side of the dark room. Ensuring to avoid the creaky spots in the floor and maneuvering around the pile of clothes by the bed, he lets out a heavy sigh of relief, and quietly sits on his twin sized mattress. However, before he can relax, he hears the fast paced and heavy footsteps of his mother coming from down the hall.

"Shit man, it's like she can smell me from a mile away."

His door bursts open with a loud thud and his mother Iris comes storming into the room with a sandal in hand. Without asking any questions, she rears her arm back and starts to quickly smack him on the back of his head.

"You've been going out after dark and trying to sneak in, again!? You think I can't hear you or even see you walking down the street dummy!?"

"Mama stop! You know I have trouble sleeping, I was just walking around trying to clear my head!"

"Boy don't you lie to your mama! Wearing all black like some criminal! Uh Uh!"

She stops for a moment to catch her breath and leans against the wall before continuing.

"What did I tell you about looking for trouble? I am your mama and I can see that you've had a death wish even since your sister disappeared!"

Feeling the sting of truth in his mother's words, Jake stands in frustration and yells, "Look! I'm a grown man now, and I'll do what I want! If I want to sneak around the streets all night looking for my sister, I will!"

Not impressed with his so-called manly attitude, Jake's mother takes a step back and crosses her arms in disappointment.

"Well, you damn sure haven't been paying any bills like a grown man would! Baby, you're twenty-two years old and still don't have a job, and it's been four long and agonizing years since your sister disappeared."

Noticing his expression become gloomy, she unfolds her arms and takes a calmer stance while looking Jake in his dark brown eyes and saying, "I know it hurts, and even I cry from time to time, but baby, we have to move forward."

A single tear runs down Jake's cheek, and he nods his head in agreement as he reaches out and tightly hugs his mother.

"Now come on, you got a call late last night when you were out. That law firm you applied to wanted to set up an interview and I told them you were available today around noon. So go take a shower and I'll make you some pancakes."

Wiping the tears from his face he says, "Thank you mama, I'll go get ready."

An hour or so goes by and Jake finds himself downstairs, sitting in front of a small plate of blueberry pancakes. Without any hesitation, he slings the mustard yellow tie around his neck over his shoulder and begins to dig in. His mother watches him eat from a couch located in the adjoining living room and says, "Your daddy would be so proud if he could see you now. I bet he never thought his favorite suit would fit you better than it did him."

With a mouth full of syrup drenched pancakes, Jake looks up at his mother and mumbles, "Thanks mama."

"It's been almost fifteen years since we left Georgia and I thought your father was going to outlive us all. That man was as strong as an Ox, and he always worked so hard." She reaches out and touches a picture of a tall, slender, Jacobean colored man and exhales with a dreamy sigh.

Jake watches his mother and puts the last of the pancakes in his mouth, *"She's endured so much, I have to do better for her."*

Noticing him staring, she says, "Oh, I don't mean to ruin your day, baby. It's getting close to noon and you still have to catch the bus. I recommend you get moving."

Turning to look at the time on the old white stove in their tiny kitchen, Jake sees "10:32"

"You're right, I've got to get going. I love you and I'll see you after."

Dropping the clothes she started folding back into her white laundry basket, she waves her hands at her fleeing son and says, "Here, I've been saving this. It was your fathers, and he used to carry this everywhere."

Turning from the door, Jake looks to his mother and watches as she reaches down behind the old mint green love seat in the living room and comes up with a light brown leather briefcase.

"Now, this is really leather, mind you. Don't lose it or leave it on the bus. I want you to look as professional as possible for your interview. After all, this is the first time you've gotten one with such a prestigious company."

He stands admiring with eyes wide and mouth agape, while reaching out with both hands to take the case with the utmost care. Running his jittery fingers over the golden colored spindle number locks on both sides, he exclaims, "Oh my God, thank you mama!"

She reaches up and places one hand on the shoulder of his baby blue suit. "Now go out there and prove to me that you really can take care of yourself. I want to hear all about it when you get back. Now go."

Not daring to argue with his mom, Jake gives her a closed mouth smile and turns for the door. Hearing the soft sobs and sniffles of his mother behind him, he grabs the handle and closes the front door of their apartment in a slow and silent manner.

Pulling out his phone to check the time, he starts to quicken his pace as he sees, 11:05.

"Oh shit! I better run!"

He can see the bus stop in the distance with passengers filing in one by one and quickens his pace to a full out sprint, ensuring the bus won't have a chance to depart without him.

"Damn bus isn't supposed to show up until 11:10."

The last of the people in line make their way on the bus with Jake just thirty feet away. He begins to panic and accidentally drops the suitcase, and with a large bounce it lands

on the old cracked asphalt road and bursts open. Scrambling to
pick it up, he begins to sweat and his breathing becomes
labored.

"Damn it!"

Jumbles of old paperwork and pens fall from the case and
Jake looks to the bus with a growing sense of dread. Scrapping
as much as he can into the case, he lifts it from the worn asphalt
and starts sprinting for the doors. Reaching them, with his
undershirt coming undone and right shoelace untied, he looks
up to see an older alabaster colored man with silver hair
looking back at him.

With a large smile, he says, "I wasn't going to leave you son.
Looks to me that you've got somewhere to be."

"Thank you so much sir! I've been left before, that's why I
panicked," Jake says with a heavy exhale while wiping the sweat
from his upper lip.

Looking in the long mirror above himself, the bus driver
says, "Go ahead and take a seat. Seems to me that there's one all
the way in the back with your name on it."

Nodding to the older gentleman, Jake makes his way to the
back of the dirty, graffiti filled bus, and takes a seat after being
eyeballed by over half of the people sitting nearby. He takes the
time to adjust his shirt and readjust his tie before looking down
towards the old leather suitcase. "Shit dad, I'm sorry."
Unclipping the locks of the case, he opens it and starts to
organize what's left of the paperwork inside. Old news clipping
with his sister's face litter the interior and Jake pauses, staring
at them with stirring emotions. Flipping through clipping after

6

clipping of missing persons ads, he stops to read the headline of one.

"Young woman's disappearance presumably linked to gang activity in the Central Park area." "That's a crock of shit!" he shouts out, causing nearby passengers to turn and look, but only for a moment before they go back to their mobile devices.

Angry at the news article clipping, he tosses it back into the case and slams the lid closed. Now feeling anger bubbling inside, he turns to look at the dark and dense and overcrowded city before him and gets lost in thought.

Thirty minutes fly by and the bus driver yells out, "Broadway, coming up!"

Standing and staring at the briefcase in his hand, he waits for the bus to halt before walking down the aisle to the front. Lethargically making his way out the doors and into the loud and busy city street, he looks up and sees a large glass and metal building standing before him.

"Alright, time to go to the 27th floor." he says, checking his watch and noticing the time, 11:43.

Widening his eyes and feeling his heart racing once again, he hastens his pace and pushes through the thick glass double paned doors leading to the large lobby. Walking with ferocity through a mile of white marble tiles towards the elevators, he notices a large man in an all-gray suit bearing down upon him.

Deciding not to turn and look he continues on his course when all of a sudden, he feels a large hand wrap around his inner elbow, "Are you in the right building?" the large man says in a high-pitched voice.

Turning to look at the security guard for the first time, Jake notices a thick black mustache on top of a nonexistent upper lip, attached to a sunburned man with beady blue eyes.

"Yes sir. I have an interview with the McDanny and Sons law firm at noon."

Looking Jake up and down the man says, "No funny business boy. Better get going if you want to make it on time. You'll find them on the 27th floor."

Scrunching his eyebrows at the security guard, Jake rips his arm away and mumbles, "Gee thanks for wasting my time" before walking to the elevators and pushing the button. Tick, tick, tick of the clock nearby bounces around Jake's ear canal as he impatiently waits by the elevator doors and notices the security guard watching nearby.

"*What the hell is this guy's problem?*"

The doors open and a chime lets Jake know that it's time to go. He rushes to board the elevator and pushes the button for the 27th floor, and stares back at the security guard practically breathing down his neck. Second's pass and the doors close, allowing Jake to take a breath by himself. Pulling out his phone and looking at the time, he mumbles, "Already 11:58." Anticipation grows as Jake passes floor by floor on his way up, and he begins to tap his foot as his patience wears thin. At last, the elevator reaches the desired floor and Jake exits the doors with haste. Upon stepping out, he comes across a young ghostly woman with bright red hair, an expressionless face, and eyes like daggers, staring back at him from behind a tall cherry colored desk.

"Yes sir-" she pauses to look him up and down before continuing, "Can I help you?"

"Yes ma'am, I'm supposed to have an interview at noon with Mr. McDanny."

Looking down at her computer, she clicks away with her mouse and says, "What's your name?"

"It's Jake Costley, ma'am."

Grumbling at his response, she says, "I see you here. Go take a seat over to your left and wait for your name to be called. I'm also going to add a note in the system about your tardiness."

Lashing back without any thought, he says, "It's exactly noon, if anything, I'm right on time."

Not even bothering to look up, she says once again, "You can find your seat over to your left. They'll call your name when they're ready," and continues to click away on her computer.

Allowing his shoulder to slump in defeat, he turns from the red-haired woman and makes his way to the four navy blue cloth chairs lining a blank white wall. Sliding into the seat and placing his suitcase between his feet, he lets out a low sigh of annoyance and places his palm against his chin.

Staring at a small clock mounted on another blank wall across the room, he shifts in his seat as the minutes tick by, and he tries to reassure himself that he has made the right choice, *"Don't Move. I need to make mama proud. I need to help her with the bills. Just take a breath."*

Sitting straight in his seat, he lifts his chest and takes a large inhale of the stale office air and blows it out in an effort to

9

steady his nerves. Just then a door to his left abruptly opens and two olive-colored men, one younger and one older, in fancy gray pinstripe suits, come out of the conference room laughing and bantering with an escalated level of excitement.

Shaking hands, the older man gives the younger man a pat on the shoulder and says, "I look forward to speaking with my sons about bringing you on. I'll give you a call with an update soon enough, my boy."

"Thank you, sir, I hope to hear from you soon."

The two men smile as they part ways and the older gentleman waves one last time before turning and locking eyes with Jake. In an instant, his mood dies down and his face becomes serious, "You must be Mr. Costley. Pam at the front desk told me you were tardy."

Standing from his chair and grabbing his suitcase, Jake begins to say, "Actually sir, I arrived-"

"No one likes excuses, young man. Come into my office and we will get started."

Not knowing what else to say, Jake nods his head and follows the older man into a carpeted office space with a large oak desk and dozens of plaques and pictures littering the walls.

Feeling a little intimidated, Jake takes a large gulp of his saliva and stands next to a tan leather chair as the man makes his way around his oversized desk.

"Take a seat young man, and we can begin."

"Yes sir."

Lowering himself into the leather chair and listening to the loud creaking noises he produces with every movement, Jake

begins to speak, "Thank you for the opportunity sir, and thank you for allowing me the last-minute interview."

Still staring at Jake with questioning eyes, the older man says, "My name is Mr. McDanny, not sir. Pam says she spoke to a nice woman on the phone who described you perfectly for the job. Looking at you now, I wasn't expecting you to be-" he pauses.

Feeling the air tension around him, Jake shifts in his seat, waiting for the closure of this man's sentence as he observes his close-cropped salt and pepper colored hair.

"So young," the man finishes with a fake half smile.

Making no comment, Jake peers at Mr. McDanny with a steely expression, and allows him to continue.

"At any rate, the position was filled previous to your arrival. So, I regret to inform you that I will be unable to help you with employment at this time."

Trying to hide his irritation, Jake replies in a tranquil tone, "I don't understand Mr. McDanny. I just heard you tell the other gentleman that a decision hadn't been made yet.... sir"

Sitting up in his chair uneasily, Mr. McDanny says, "Well uh, that was for another position, not the counselor's assistant position you are applying for. I can direct you to a few other firms that might be more of your style if you'd like."

"More my style?"

Moving his hand up and down as if pointing to Jake's appearance, Mr. McDanny says, "You know....some people that you may relate to more."

Shooting straight up from his chair with fire in his eyes, Jake exclaims, "Say no more, I understand!"

Without even waiting for Mr. McDanny's response, he grabs his father's briefcase and asserts, "Good day, sir!" and storms out of the office.

Glaring at the red woman behind the front desk as she scrambles for her phone, Jake smashes the call button to the elevator and stands in silence, broadening in his anger. Hearing the chime of the elevator, he takes a step forward just as the door opens and quickly presses for the ground level.

With the doors closed and standing alone, he yells, "What the hell is wrong with these people?! I have never seen such disrespect!"

The elevator door chimes once again and Jake now finds himself on the ground level, and to his surprise the security guard is waiting nearby.

"I thought I told you not to cause any trouble, boy! I just got the call that you were yelling and scaring those poor office workers! You better leave the building now before I make you leave!"

"Don't worry, I'll show myself out of this racist rat's nest!" he fires back.

The smug look on the security guard's face drops, and he looks at Jake with a menacing grin as he steps forward with one hand extended. Not wanting this overgrown, lip less fool to be near him, Jake instinctively reacts and smashes his briefcase into the security guard's face. His nose erupts into a volcanic shower of deep red, and Jake's adrenaline spikes. With his heartbeat pulsating throughout his head, he takes his now blood-stained briefcase and runs for the front door. In a failed attempt, the guard reaches for Jake's jacket but falls straight on his face, just before passing out.

With a smile, and his legs feeling weightless, Jake runs right out the front door, and like a shot of light, down the street.

An unknown amount of time passes as Jake continues to let his legs guide him home. The adrenaline starts to wear off, and he now feels an immense amount of pain in his feet and an intense burn in his lungs. Coming to a screeching halt in the middle of the sidewalk opposite his apartment building, Jake puts his hands above his head and attempts to take large breaths in and out while walking in circles.

Feeling winded, yet exhilarated, he shouts, "What the fuck just happened!?"

"Damn that felt sooooo good! I should have just done that when he first grabbed me!"

An intense thirst strikes Jake, and he lowers his arms to his side and begins to cross the street while still trying to catch his breath. Struggling to gain his composure, he makes his way through the first floor of the apartment building and tiptoes up the steps to the second.

He looks to the briefcase he still clings to, and with hints of vanity in his voice, says, "*Bet dad never saw that happening with his favorite case.*"

Letting out a small chuckle as he approaches the door of his mother's apartment. He lifts himself tall and fixes his father's old suit as best he can. Feeling satisfied, he inserts his key and unlocks the door.

Bloody Interventions

The street lights of this never sleeping city do little against the bright illumination of the small 24-hour storefronts lining the thin downtown roads of Jake's neighborhood. Making his way past the stores and out of his neighborhood with as much stealth as he can manage, he begins patrolling the streets bordering Central Park as he has many nights before. Although he doesn't know what kind of clues to look for, he now understands the impulse behind his decisions. Pulling his hands from his hoodie, he makes two fists and envisions the spurting blood of the security guard. Remembering the surge of energy and the lack of pain with his adrenaline rush, he tries to assure himself that it was a fluke, "I did not like hurting him. I simply let my anger get the best of me. You will not make this a habit."

Looking up into the dark park before him, a memory stirs and a cold chill runs down his spine.

"Come on Jake, Mama's going to be mad if we don't get home before sundown," Imani calls out.

"Ya, ya, let her get mad. I'm a man now. Eighteen years old and as strong as Daddy."

"Oh, you're a tough guy now? I didn't realize those string bean arms of yours bulked up when you turned eighteen. That's some super power you have."

"Man shut up! You know daddy's been taking me to a boxing club near the apartment since I was sixteen, and I've become ten times stronger than I used to be, so you better watch out!"

Pointing to the descending sun, Imani says, "Well unless we get home before sundown, Mama's going to kill us before you ever get a chance to set foot in the ring."

"Why don't we just cut through the park then. All we have to do is get towards 72nd street and it'll be all pavement from there. I really don't want to walk all the way to 79th street traverse, Imani."

Staring off into the dark spots of Central park, Imani feels a ball forming in her stomach.

"I don't know Jake. You know the majority of crime in the park is near sundown and after dark."

Flapping his arms around like a chicken, Jake begins to cluck and sings, "Buck Buck Buck, Chicken, Buck Buck Buck!"

Imani flails her arm around and catches Jake right on the back of his head, making a smacking sound. They both begin to laugh as Jake clutches the already visible welt, and shakes his fist in defiance.

"Fine! But let's make it quick! Since you're so strong now, I bet you won't mind running through the park," she challenges.

"Oh, you're on! Last one to the other side has to do the dishes for the next ten years!" Jake yells out, already running through a darkening section of the wood line.

Keeping pace with Jake, Imani's footsteps can be heard as the pair make their way through light and dark spots of the park, racing into the dusk of another day.

Jake's breathing intensifies, and he yells out, "Maybe I shouldn't have said let's run!"

"Ya well you asked for-Ah!" Imani yells out mid-sentence.

Coming to a grinding halt, Jake turns, expecting to see his sister clutching her ankle in pain but instead sees a man standing over her limp body.

"Yo man, what the fuck is your problem?!" He shouts out. Raising both fists he takes a step toward the attacker and prepares for a fight, but instead is met with a heavy thump against the back of his head.

Now laying on the ground with increasingly blurred vision, he reaches out for his sister as she is being dragged away by two men in dark hoodies and hoarsely says, "Imani," just as he blacks out.

Screaming fills Jake's ears as he stands near a forested section of the park and without hesitation, he begins to sprint into the dark wood line. Listening for another scream to orient himself, he slows to a trot. Sure enough, as loud as the first, a scream rings out. Quickening his pace, he soon finds himself standing on a wooden bridge arching over a small creek. He

17

looks up to the sky, with a long deep breath, and begins to listen once more.

This time he hears a man yelling in a hushed tone, "Shut you fucking suck bitch and stop kicking! This won't hurt too much!"

His body temperature skyrockets, and a surge of energy runs through his body. Lunging from his standing position and darting about twenty yards (ca. 18 m) down the thin trail before him, he sees a man standing over a younger woman in the bright light of the moon.

Little runs through Jake's mind as he fully spears the man in the back with his large shoulder and violently throws him to the ground, yelling, "I'll kill you, you piece of shit! Get off Imani!"

With red fury clouding his vision and mind, he throws massive fist after massive fist against the man's face until his sun burnt leathery skin becomes covered in a thick blanket of blood. Feeling the man's body go completely limp, he raises his hands, cups them together, and delivers one final blow. Crunching noises fill the air and a feeling of exhaustion washes over Jake as he falls to the side. Lying next to the bloody mess and staring at the moon, he exclaims, "Ma'am, are you alright?"

Hearing no response, he grabs at the ground until he finds a nearby root and uses it to pull himself up. Sitting in the fetal position nearby, the young woman, as pale as the moon itself, stares back with terror in her eyes.

"H-h-he was going to rape me!" She sobbingly exclaims, staring at the shadowed puddle of a man before her.

"Don't you worry Ma'am; I won't let him touch you ever again. I'm going to call the cops, and we'll get you home."

He struggles to stand with strained breaths, and feels a throbbing pain shoot through his hands as he looks at the motionless man.

Pulling his phone from his back pocket and turning on the light, he takes a step away from the body and turns towards the young woman. Panic swells in his breast, and he looks to his hands and sees the blood dripping from between his knuckles while saying,

"Oh my god, I think I killed him!"

Seeing the look on Jake's now illuminated face, the fearful girl reaches up and grabs his bloody hand, "You saved me. I can't thank you enough."

Looking down at the young woman's hand interlaced in his, he takes a deep breath, lifts the phone and dials for the police. The phone rings twice before the operator answers and says, "911, what is your emergency?"

Jake swallows his saliva and in a high-strung tone says, "We need help in Central Park, I think I just killed a man."

Unintentional Fame

Refusing to let go, the young woman from the park grips Jake's hand with all her might. He comforts her with an arm around her shoulder. Able to see her in the well-lit police station, Jake realizes just how young she really is. No more than sixteen years of age, with dark hair and pale skin, he looks into her frightened eyes and begins to wonder why she was in the park after sundown.

Giving her a good squeeze of reassurance, he says, "It'll be alright now. No one here is going to lay a finger on you unless you say so."

Small tears fall from her eyes as she tucks her face into his chest. With an impatient look starting to show, he waves to the Desk Sergeant nearby and mouths, "We've been here for two hours, sir."

The chubby cheeked police officer looks at Jake through his stern face and judging eyes and exclaims, "I told you. The detectives will be with you shortly!" He looks back to the stack of paperwork on his desk and continues to organize them methodically. Jake lets out a grunt of frustration and leans his head back against the glass divider separating them from the cubicles behind. Allowing his exhaustion to set in, he closes his eyes and begins to nod off.

What feels like moments pass and Jake is awakened with a jerk. Peering through tired eyes, he now sees on a clock in the distance that another hour has passed since he last spoke to the Desk Sergeant. Without change, the police officer is still organizing paperwork. Shaking his head at the man, Jake looks down to the young woman and sees her peacefully sleeping in his lap.

"*She's just a damn kid. No one deserves to go through a trauma like that.*" Raising his hands and looking at the purple hue of his knuckles, his face goes blank.

"*I killed that man. I shouldn't have done that. No, it had to be done or else he would be back on the streets.*"

Lowering his hands and looking down the hall in front of him, he sees a slender man in regular clothing walking toward him. Waiting for the man to get closer to ensure he is indeed bound for them; he reaches down with a gentle hand and shakes the young girl awake.

"Hey. I think the detective is ready."

She grumbles and pushes herself to a seated position while rubbing her eyes and the slender gentleman stops but a few feet from them while looking at some paperwork.

"I take it you two are Jake Costley, and Meana Crane?"

In unison, they nod their heads in agreement and follow him down a long white hallway with old worn ivory-colored tiles for a floor. He gestures for Meana to enter a plain gray room with an all-metal table and two metal chairs. She hesitates to enter and stops at the threshold of the doorway to look at Jake.

Noticing her fear begin to rise again, he comforted her by saying, "Don't worry Meana, I'll be right across the hall. If anything happens, just yell my name and I'll bust through the wall."

Jake pretends to break through a block wall like The Incredible Hulk with his hands waving above his head, and she lets out a small giggle. Turning away from him and following the detective, she steps through the doorway and takes a seat on the cold metal chair as Jake makes his way to a similar room across the hall. With both doors open, he looks to his right and sees Meana fidgeting with both hands under the table.

"I hope they go easy on her."

A different man enters his room and closes the door behind himself, cutting off Jake's line of sight with Meana. He looks at the new detective and notices his nice black suit and slicked back hairstyle and more so, the badge upon his leather belt that says, "FBI."

Feeling his nerves begin to twitch, Jake shifts in his chair and places both of his hands above the table. Unsure as to why an FBI agent would take interest in this case, he decides it best to ensure his hands are clearly in sight. Dropping a large file onto the table with a loud slapping sound, the FBI agent lets out a sigh and takes a seat across Jake.

"Alright young man, I can tell you're nervous. I've done this a million times and I can always tell when someone has spotted my badge. Take a deep breath, I'm not here to arrest you."

Still, a little unsure of the agent, Jake remains stiff in his chair. Leaning forward while staring at the large manila folder,

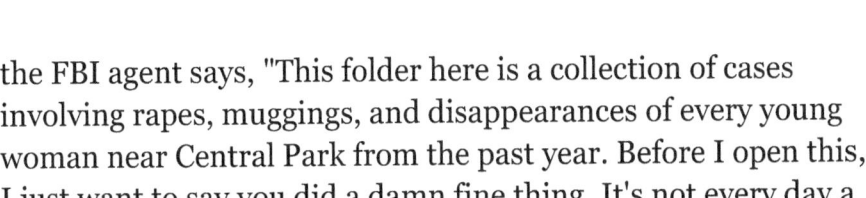

the FBI agent says, "This folder here is a collection of cases involving rapes, muggings, and disappearances of every young woman near Central Park from the past year. Before I open this, I just want to say you did a damn fine thing. It's not every day a young lady is fortunate enough to be rescued from an attacker."

Unsure whether he can trust the agent or not, he leans backward in his chair and crosses his arms. Spreading his feet and placing them flat on the ground for comfort, he asks, "So, why am I here?"

The nameless agent flips the folder wide open and the images within make Jake's eyes widen in disbelief. Bloody bodies, crying faces, torn clothing, and even pictures of shoes and jewelry that were left at the crime scenes. Looking away from the photos, Jake says, "What is this?"

Observing Jake with a hard gaze, the agent says, "These are the victims of the man you killed. We have been tracking his movements for a year now. He is a serial rapist, with a serious attitude problem. He never cares about leaving his DNA behind, but with the amount of homeless people roaming the streets at any given point, he virtually became invisible to the system."

Clearing his throat before continuing to debrief Jake, "Unfortunately no online presence means no virtual tracking. However, you did help me close this case and because of it, there are going to be some reporters waiting for you outside the station. They've caught the scent of your story and like vultures they're descending. I recommend that you keep your story short and without too much detail. Officially, you and I never spoke."

Nodding to the FBI agent in agreement, Jake whispers, "Thanks for the advice."

Standing from his chair, the agent makes his way to the door with his thick folder in hand and swings it open with a smooth flick of his wrist. Turning to look at Jake, he nods and gives him a smirk before exiting the room. Taking that as his cue to leave, Jake rises from his metal chair and makes his way back towards the front entrance of the police station. Hesitating a moment to pause in front of Meana's closed detention room door, he says, "Stay strong kiddo," and makes for the entrance. Noticing a small group of people with cameras standing on the other side of the automatic glass double doors of the station, he takes a deep breath and exits. Flashes of light fill the air and at least four separate reporters stick their cameras and microphones in his face.

"Mr. Costley! Rebecca Jenkins from The Press for the People! Why were you in the park after sundown!?"

Before he can answer, another reporter asks a second question, "Reports have come in that you killed the attacker in the park! How do you feel about murdering a man to save that girl's life!?"

Completely caught off guard by the questions, Jake takes a step back and feels his head begin to spin.

"I- I don't know."

Pushing forward to fill the void between them, the reporters continue to pummel Jake with questions as their cameras never cease to film and flash. Feeling panic slither it's way under his skin, Jake turns from the reporters and begins to sprint into the darkness.

"Wait Mr. Costley, we have a few more questions!" Can be heard in the distance but Jake doesn't dare turn to look back. Running with ferocity into the night, Jake's heart pounds like a set of war drums in the dark. Crawling in the back of his mind just loud enough to be heard over his heavy breathing is a hushed voice saying, *"We are one. Now and forever."*

Feeling the Pressure

 "Wake your ass up Jake! What did I tell you about sleeping in late? I'm about to take these blackout curtains from you and let the neighbors look through! We'll see how long you sleep then!"

"Mama! Please!" he says with half opened eyes.

"Don't Mama me! You think saving the skinny girl means you don't have to keep looking for a job? It's been over a month now and all your fame has already faded! You know this city; they find something else of interest before they even finish the article with your name in it!"

Grunting out of frustration, Jake pulls the blanket higher over his face. Seeing him trying to hide from the sun, Iris reaches down and rips the blanket off of him.

"Mama!" he exclaims, flopping around the bed like a child.

Without hesitation, she slips off her sandal and goes to work. Loud slaps can be heard down the block and within seconds, Jake finds himself up and in the shower.

Trudging down the steep flight of stairs leading to their small kitchen he asks, "What's for breakfast?"

Firing back with a scowling look, Iris says, "Breakfast? You mean lunch you bum?"

Still, lethargically making his way into the kitchen, he shrugs his shoulders and slumps in the old wooden chair at the oval dinner table. Pulling his phone from his pocket and unlocking the screen, he begins to scroll through his social media page. Message after message litter his inbox, and he reads through them with a smirk on his face:

"Good job my man, cleaning up the city!"

"You're so hot!"

"Praying for you and yours!"

Though his smile quickly fades as he reads on:

"Fuck you! No better than the other thugs on the corner!"

"A killer murdering a rapist, no better than animals in a zoo!"

Jake throws the phone on the kitchen table and lets out a loud grunt just as the phone makes an even louder thud.

Scrambling eggs and chopped bacon in an old cast iron pan on the stove, Iris just about jumps out of her skin while yelping, "What the fuck!?" and following up with, "I'm sorry lord, please forgive me."

Turning with bulging eyes and veins protruding from her forehead, she looks to Jake with her wooden spatula held high but then pauses, looking at his gloomy face.

Glancing at his phone, she says, "You can't keep reading those messages baby. For every person that loves you, there are three more filled with hate and envy. People are a flawed nasty bunch. Personally, I think they all need Jesus."

27

"Right Mama, Jesus is going to come swooping down to save us all. I'm going to go for a walk."

He stands from the table and briskly makes his way to the door with his phone in hand, leaving Iris speechless by the stove. "I'll see you in an hour or so, I just need to clear my head," and closes the door.

Feeling the weight of depression, he makes his way out of the building and chokes back tears. He rounds the corner leading to the alley nearby and stops to lean against the wall. Clutching his face with his hands and feeling his eyes begin to burn, a steady stream of tears pours forth. Images of that night in the park begin to flash through his mind. Darkness, spurts of blood, the smell of mud, and blinding red. The sound of crunching of bones plays over and over, as he places his hands over his ears in an attempt to muffle the sounds.

"Go away!" he growls as he feels control slipping through his fingers.

Seconds away from a total meltdown, he is interrupted by the loud ringing of his cellphone. Being broken out of his episode, he looks in confusion at the bright screen and sees a name he never expected, Caster Roderick. In disbelief, he presses the small green circle on his touch screen and quizzically says, "Cas?"

A friendly and familiar voice comes over the other end, "Hey brother, I've been meaning to reach out."

"Nah man, it's alright. Um, how have you been? We were worried about you." he tries to sound calm and collected as he wipes the tears from his face.

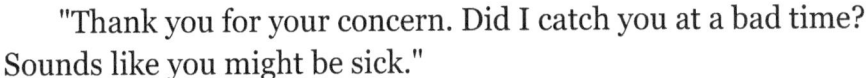

"Thank you for your concern. Did I catch you at a bad time? Sounds like you might be sick."

" Nah, nah man, you just caught me after a long run."

"That's my man, still working the bag at Bennie's and running everyday like your pops wanted, right?"

Not wanting to come off as a failure, Jake lies, "You know it man. Gotta keep the ladies satisfied. Anyway, what's up with you?"

"Nothing much bro, just wanted to call and check in with you. I just got back to the states about a month ago and to my surprise, there you were in the paper. Said you saved a young woman and killed her attacker in self-defense. That takes some serious guts my man."

"Thanks Cas, it was all that training just kicking in."

"That's great! That's not the only reason I'm calling though. So, I've been making mad cash out of the country doing B-rated films and bro, I'm in need of a bad-ass brother like you for my next action/horror film."

Puzzled at this random call and even more random job offer, Jake questions, "I don't know man. I haven't seen you since Imani. My Mama, I mean mom, would probably flip if I just left the country for some sketchy spot on a movie set."

"I hear you, and I totally see where you're coming from, but check this out. I will pay for your tickets and I'll even pay for your lodging. If that's not enough, I'll even spot you a grand up front."

Little thought runs through his mind as he places his hand on the back of his head and lets the fluttering in his heart answer, "Alright bro, I could really use a break from this shit hole. Oh? You said tickets?"

"Ya bro, that's the best part, I'll even bring your mom along too. She can watch her boy in action and I might even get her a spot on set too."

"Holy shit man, I'm in, whether mom says yes or no. Where's the movie being shot at?"

A second of static and hesitation fills the line as Caster can be heard drawing a breath, "Bro, it's in Panama. The land of beautiful jungles and even finer women!"

Anticipation Climbs

Looking at the high white ceiling tiles of LaGuardia airport, Jake sighs and cracks his neck with both hands as he and his mama, Iris, wait in line for their turn with security.

"This is outrageous! You'd think after so many years of flying, humans would have developed a better way of doing this."

"Hush boy. You think because you saved that girl, they should part this sea of bodies and let you walk on through?" Iris says in a low yet aggressive tone.

Pursing his lips, Jake slumps his shoulders and allows his carry-on bag to slip off his shoulder and rest on the floor. Passenger after passenger goes through the customs gate and Jake can feel his patience growing thin. Tapping his foot faster as the seconds go by, Iris looks at him and slaps his arm with her passport.

"Look here young man. I did not agree to fly to some random jungle in the middle of God knows where, so I can be stuck with your impatience and the, *I'm too good for waiting attitude*. This is a huge opportunity for you and maybe, just maybe, we won't have to struggle with those damn bills, or those annoying collection calls anymore."

31

Rolling his head from left to right, Jake looks at his mother and sees her devious smile as she mentions money and says in a disappointed tone, "Mama, I don't think I'm going to be getting paid very much. Caster said it was a B rated film. I just want out of that city and to see Caster after four years of wondering what he's been up to since-" he pauses and looks away, "Imani."

Iris says with a knitted brow, "Jake I swear to baby Jesus himself, if this is about your sister, I'm going to lose my mind."

Glancing off into the distant rows of passengers standing in food court lines on the other side of security, Jake falls silent.

"I should have known. You're just like your Daddy. Spending every night on the street looking for imaginary clues." Waving her hands around as if dispersing a foul smell around her, she continues, "He'd still be here today, standing beside you instead of me. Cheering you on, if he hadn't been walking those cursed streets. In the end, we lost two souls instead of one, and I will not watch you make the same mistakes."

Jake smacks his lips and continues gazing into the distance. "I'm not like Daddy. I watch from afar. I never walked up to some strange bum on the street, interrogating them like they were criminals and that's why I've lived longer prowling the streets than he did. " Hesitating before continuing, he says, "Plus, I'm not drowning my sorrows in copious amounts of alcohol."

He glaringly turns towards his mother and feels his heart drop as a single tear falls from her eye and her lower lip begins to quiver. Turning from her son and looking towards the airport personnel on duty, she sniffles and says, "Your right baby. He was a damn fool who wouldn't listen but that doesn't excuse you and sure as hell doesn't make you any better than him."

With her closing statement on the subject at hand, the two-stand side by side in awkward silence as they continue to progress through the overly crowded area of security with their luggage in hand.

Finally reaching the other side of airport security after waiting an hour, they push through the sea of people standing around the main common area looking lost.

"Caster said he'd be meeting us at the terminal and that he got us first class tickets."

Struggling to pull her deep purple suitcase behind herself and wheezing while trying to keep pace with Jake, Iris struggles to say, "Wow, I didn't realize he had cash on hand like that."

"According to him, making B-rated films can generate some serious money with the right viewers. Plus, we are in desperate need of some money. If all else fails, we'll get a free trip out of NYC for two weeks."

Jake blazes a path through the constant flow of tourists and business people with shoulder checks and pushes, and lets out a grunt of irritation. For him the brisk walk feels as if it's taking them a lifetime. Leaving his mama on the verge of collapse about twenty paces behind, he looks around their crowded terminal in confusion. Unable to spot Caster, he paces back and forth in the main walkway.

"Looking for someone?" a familiar voice says from the men's restroom entrance behind Jake.

Whipping around, Jake exclaims, "Cas!"

"The one and only. Stand still, let me take a look at you." Inspecting Jake from head to toe and circling him like a vulture, Caster nods his head and says, "Looks like you've been busy training. You look tougher than I remember."

Flexing his biceps with two lifted arms and his carry-on dangling, he vainly says, "Just pumping some iron at the gym is all."

Meanwhile, a huffing and puffing Iris finally catches up to them and before she can catch her breath, Caster makes his way to her and squeezes the last of the air from her lungs.

"It's so good to see you Mrs. Costley!"

Struggling to breath, she pats him on the shoulder and says through heavy panting, "Baby, you know you can call me Iris. You were part of our family for so long that we were just as worried when you disappeared too."

Releasing his grip, he merrily says, "Well no worries, I'm back and ready to share the wealth of knowledge and cash!" Waving a small stack of bills under her nose.

"As promised. Jake, here is the one thousand dollars upfront."

Snatching the money from his hands, Jake looks around and whispers, "Have you lost your mind? Did you forget how dangerous flashing cash in New York can be?"

Putting his hands to his mouth in a playful manner, Caster says, "Oops, wouldn't want someone to come and challenge big Jake."

"Not funny bro. I've never been one for a fight and I still don't want to start any issues."

"Alright, alright you two. Enough playing around. I need to rest my old bones," Iris says, while walking away and be-lining towards a singular open spot by their terminal.

Both Caster and Jake watch Iris take her seat in the distance and then turn towards each other. Caster puts a hand on Jake's shoulder and says, "It's great to see you brother. Let's go find a seat and I'll fill you in on the big plans for the movie."

Land of Confusion

Jake's ears perk up as the ringing of a yellow nicotine-stained telephone fills the air, and he opens his eyes to a darkened morning. *Who could be calling this damn early?*

"Jake, for the love of Christ, get that phone" Iris grumbles from beneath the pillow that lay atop her face.

He reaches across his body to the low and faded nightstand between their two small twin sized beds, and lifts the receiver to groggily say, "Hello?"

"Rise and shine Jakey boy! Time to head out for the location of the shoot and to capture some amazing photos on the way! I hope you brought a camera!" says Caster with irritating amounts of excitement.

"Yo, what time is it?"

"It's 3:30 brother! Get yourself together and meet me downstairs in the lobby no later than 4:15. Got it?"

"Ya, I got it." and he aggressively slams the receiver.

"Ma!?"

"What, boy!?"

"Apparently it's time to rise and shine."

"What time is it?"

"You don't want to know. Let's just get moving and see where we go from there."

Rolling out of bed and to their feet, Jake and Iris lethargically gather their belongings and prepare for an exciting day of traveling through the thick jungles to the filming grounds. Still feeling the tightness of sleeping on a twin sized mattress filled with an assortment of lumps working its way out of his back, Jake puts his hands above his head and yawns obnoxiously.

"Boy, you act like you're fifty years old. Psh, you just wait until you're my age. I can't believe I let you talk me into this trip. Here I am thinking I'm about to sleep in a five-star hotel-"

"Mama please don't start. Let's just get down stairs and get some breakfast."

4:05 strikes the small black and white clock hanging on the wall behind the receptionist desk in the lobby of the rundown hotel. Jake, and Iris drag their bags nearby with loud scraping noises echoing off the empty hallway walls.

Caster watches from a distance and snickers to himself while they make their way down the hall and yells out, "Man, if I had known you made such a great zombie, I would have budgeted for that film instead!"

Smacking his lips, and staring through bloodshot eyes, Jake asks, "What's for breakfast?"

"Thought you'd ask. So I took the liberty of securing you some protein bars and your favorite..... Water."

"This motherfucker!"

"What do you mean, took the liberty?" asks Jake, now wide-eyed and annoyed.

"Oh bro, I forgot to tell you. This hotel doesn't have breakfast services like the American hotels. They're not quite that fancy yet."

Iris, looking up from the floor, shouts, "Say what!?"

Trying to hide his devious smirk, Caster lifts the protein bars and bottled water to chest level while shrugging his shoulders and saying, "I promise you won't be so angry once we reach the jungle areas and the sun begins to rise. There are some views that most tourists would die to see."

"Alright man, whatever. Let's just get moving, I guess. So where to now, big shot?"

Caster passes the protein bars and water to Jake and while looking at their luggage he lifts his right hand and snaps his fingers. As if appearing from nowhere, two very slender Panamanian gentlemen step from behind the large columns nearby and grab their suitcases.

Unable to understand what Caster says, in Spanish, Jake assumes it's something along the lines of, "Get their bags and load them in the car" because without hesitation, they do just that.

Impressed, Jake purses his lips and widens his eyes as he gives a bow of respect to Caster, and says,

"That was dope."

Shrugging his shoulders like it's just another ordinary day, Caster gestures to the vehicles parked out front.

"Shall we?"

Nodding his head in approval, Jake turns to his Mama and reaches for her hand. "Come on Ma, let's get this party started."

They make their way out of the hotel, and hop in two beefed-up Jeeps with a tri-color camouflage paint job.

Noticing the military appearance of the man soon to chauffeur them through the jungle, Jake turns to Caster, who is now sitting in the front seat, and asks, "Military?"

"I didn't want to scare you but, some locals can be kind of rough on tourists, and the terrain we're going to be going through needs the kind of guidance they won't dare interfere with."

Iris, sitting next to Jake in the back, worriedly reaches over and clutches at his bicep with a look of dread washing over her.

Noticing her panic in the rear passenger seat, Caster smiles and reassures her, "No worries Iris. You're in good hands. You'll see some military types in the camp we've set up, but they're just there to watch our backs."

"Ya well I don't know what scares me more. Random locals trying to rob me or weird men in uniforms watching me day and night," she snaps back.

"Mama, I'm sure Caster has done this many times before and has everything planned out. Right bro?"

"Ya man, I've done this at least two or three dozen times before. Been perfecting this setup since I left New York City years ago."

"See ma. Nothing to worry about," Jake says with a bead of sweat dripping from his brow.

Without another word, the commute to the dense forested areas of their shoot commences, and the further they get from civilization, the darker the sky becomes. Noticing the density of the night sky, Jake feels a slight chill run up his spine and places a hand on the still clutching palm of Iris.

A few hours pass as they traverse the winding, thin, and bumpy dirt roads of the Panamanian jungles, and Jake finally breaks the silence just as the sun begins to crest the canopy high above.

"You said you've done this about two or three dozen times right? What are the titles of some of your movies? For some reason it never occurred to me that I should ask."

"Ah man, you won't even know how to say the names of our movies. Most of them are in Spanish and some people here have their own dialect that's like a really mixed Spanish. None of the movies have ever been on any big-time streaming networks. My movies mostly circulate through Central and Southern America."

Looking back to Jake with a devilish smirk, he continues, "But no worry's bro. If it's getting paid, you're worried about, I guarantee you'll get exactly what I promised. The viewers here definitely spend good cash to see a decent film."

Feeling uneasy at the constant evasion of Caster's answers, Jake shoots a halfhearted smirk back and turns his gaze to the deep wood outside the vehicle.

Still gripping his mama's hand, Jake and Iris sit in silence for the remainder of the ride, and Jake internally begins to panic.

"This shit ain't right! I should have asked more questions! I shouldn't have been so desperate to find answers about Imani! Calm down Jake, he did say it would be in the deep jungles before you even got on the plane! Nothing sketch going on at all, nothing-"

The Jeep comes to a grinding and mud splattering halt as they crest a small ridge, and bear down on a row of block buildings draped with camouflage patterned canopies, and littered with men in uniforms.

A tingling sensation runs through Jake's body, and his heart begins to pound. Looking at the intimidating gathering of soldiers nearby, his mind runs wild with fear.

Jumping from the front seat and stretching his arms out wide, Caster yawns and follows up with, "Alright, time to get you guys settled in."

He turns towards Jake and Iris, and notices the paling of their complexion and wide-eyed looks. Turning to find the cause of their panic he lets out a giggle and says, "Oh come on now. These guys aren't the actual soldiers. Remember this is a giant movie set and the majority of these guys are preparing for another movie we're filming on the west side of the compound. It's a war-based film with loud explosions and glorified fire fights."

Seeing they're not convinced; he walks around the vehicle to Iris's side and escorts her out of the seat.

"Now I promised Jake that if he brought you, I would give you a special job that kept you busy while he was working."

Looking deep into her dark ocher colored eyes he asks, "Iris, are you ready to see what I'm going to pay you to do?"

Taking a few deep breaths to stabilize herself, her vision darts back and forth between his wheat-colored skin and hazel-colored eyes, and she squeaks, "Y-yes sir."

He waves Jake down and signals for him to meet near the hunter green tent set up just outside the main block building. He then walks Iris through the muddy terrain and into one of the buildings while escorting her with their arms interlocked.

Doing as Caster directed, Jake leaps from his seat and walks to the tent. Pulling back the large flap that separates the interior from the wilderness around, he can't believe his eyes. Interlocking wooden boards litter the ground, forming a makeshift walkway. On either side of the tent is a queen size spring mattress with a metal frame, smothered in beige cotton sheets. Solar powered lights dangle from the main shaft of the tent's frame, and Jake makes his way to a small table on the far end. Pressed against the back canvas of the tent, he sees mounds of paperwork with notes and scripted lines for movie ideas sitting atop the desk. Signed at the bottom right-hand corner of each page is *Caster Roderick*.

"*Damn. He's a lot more serious than I gave him credit for. Let's see what he's got planned for this film.*"

He reaches down and pinches the corner of the paper laying on top titled *Pana-Mania,* and with two fingers he begins to turn it with care. However, before he reveals the secrets within

42

the stack of paperwork, Caster flips back the canvas entryway and exclaims in a joking tone, "Oh buddy! I hope you're not trying to steal any of my ideas, Jakey boy! I better not leave that lying around!"

Releasing the page and allowing it to fall back into place, Jake whips around and says, "You know me bro. Just excited to see what's in store."

"You don't worry about that. Remember, I told you about your part at the airport. Anyway, I've got your mother set up with the communications team in the main building. She'll be sitting around all day getting paid to watch the live feeds from the cameras we have set up in the Jungles, and drinking some ice-cold beverages as we sweat. All she has to do is report when a camera goes down."

Becoming more surprised by the second. Jake allows his expression to soften and says, "I can't thank you enough. We've been having some really tough times lately and you called at the perfect moment."

Seeing a tear swell in Jake's eyes, Caster walks across the tent and firmly embraces him. Still gripping Jake with his face resting against his shoulder, Caster says, "You're like a little brother to me. I shouldn't have left your family like I did. It's just... Imani's disappearance hit me hard, and after a few months of nothing from the detectives, I just lost myself a bit."

Wiping the tears from his face and sniffling, Jake follows up with, "Ya man, I was hoping you could help me. When I saw your name on the phone, what I really saw was a chance to get some answers."

Releasing Jake and taking a step back in surprise, Caster says, "What kind of answers can I give you that you don't already have?"

"I don't know bro. I mean, you were her boyfriend since the seventh grade and if anything, you could tell me where she used to hang out when she wasn't with family."

Caster lowers his head toward the ground and lets a grim look set it. He lets out a loud sigh and convinces Jake, "Look bro, I don't know how I can help you, but I'll try. For now, let's get you settled in, and we can talk more on the subject another time."

Nodding approvingly, Jake and Caster exchange one last hug and Jake walks over to his queen-sized mattress and slumps into the springs in silence.

Traversing the Mysterious

"Wakey, wakey, eggs, and bakey!" Caster calls out from the tent entrance with two steaming mugs of coffee in hand. Rolling over and sniffing the air, Iris says with ample amounts of glee, "Is that coffee I smell?!"

"It sure is! There's also some breakfast waiting in the main facility when you're up to it."

"Lord, bless you! I'm ready to eat after all that work I put in late last night."

Grumbling from under his thin cotton blanket, Jake says, "What work? You mean sitting around watching T.V. all day?"

Interrupting before the glaring Iris can take off her slipper, Caster defends her. "Wow, not cool bro. You know that without those Cameras we can't make money on these films. No money means no payday, am I right?"

"Uhuh!" Iris agrees, looking at Jake with a spiteful grin.

Setting the cups down on a small table nearby, Caster asks, "So how was the tent? Hope the humidity didn't creep in."

"The tent is lovely Caster. It was just right in here. I'm surprised it wasn't a thousand degrees last night."

"It's the canvas material, and the interlocking wood floor we put down. They create almost like a sealed environment for the inhabitant. I actually use this tent regularly, but I decided since you guys are like family, I would sleep inside on a cot with the other actors for the time being.

"You see, Jake? I wish you had the same level of charm as Caster here. Maybe you'd have found a nice woman to take you out of that run-down apartment."

Now flipping the covers back and looking at Iris with bloodshot eyes, he exclaims, "That apartment?! Mama, did you forget that you live there too?! Also, we live in NYC, not some small town in Georgia where a southern bell can just come along and pluck my heart when she wants!"

Iris looks to Caster and asks, "So about that breakfast?"

Thirty minutes fly by, and the duo are standing in a long line for breakfast when they see Caster in the distance. He waves them to the front of the line, and Jake notices the multitude of murderous looks from the other actors. Brushing their jealousy off, he and Iris quickly make their way forward.

"You guys are funny. I told you, you're still like family and my family doesn't eat the same slop that we feed the local actors," Caster says in a hushed tone.

"I've got some eggs, bacon, and toast waiting for you through those double doors over there." He points to a set of all gray steel doors, and Iris begins to smile.

"Oh Jake. Wait until you see the set up they have hiding behind those doors."

"To be honest, my mind is only on breakfast. I'll be more excited after I eat," he whines while rubbing his stomach in a circular motion.

In a nonchalant manner, they make their way to the double doors and as they breach the threshold, Jake turns to look at the faces of the locals once more. This time though, he notices looks of pity, rather than jealousy. He scrunches his brows in confusion and then decides there is nothing further to question.

"*These people are weird.*"

Caster closes the doors behind them and turns with arms wide open, and says, "Jake, let me introduce you to the last four years of my life. This is the main area in which we film the more detailed scenes, and all of our indoor scenarios."

Looking around in amazement, Jake can see huge areas segmented and filled with gear and props for any kind of scene. Glancing from one set to another, he says, "Horror, action, martial arts, and .... Romance?" Pointing to a large bed lined with rose petals and obnoxiously pink decor.

Letting out a nervous laugh, Caster says, "We can't do blood and guts all the time, right?"

Jake shrugs his shoulders and continues to look about while Iris and Caster walk over to a long foldout table with their plates at the ready. Walking by each set with mouth agape, he becomes more and more astonished at the detail, and the hustle and bustle of the camera crews nearby.

"*These people really take their work seriously. I would have never thought so much time and effort could be sitting in the middle of some random jungle.*"

Just then, he walks up to the horror set. Torture devises lay about and stretch racks line a wall to his left. This area seems to be smaller than the others, and has a drain built into the all-white tiled floor.

"Damn! They even built a fake drain to simulate a real torture room. This shit is wild."

"Hey Jake? Why don't you come and eat? I'll show you to the costume room, and we'll get your first set of scenes out of the way after breakfast. You won't have many parts, and we should be able to finish up within a few days of filming"

He turns to face Caster, and notices Iris already sitting at the table with a mouth full of eggs. She looks up from her plate and gestures for him to follow suit. He does as she instructs, and they sit around the table, laughing and feasting on a plethora of eggs, bacon, and toast.

Time melts by for them, and Caster looks to his happy guests and says, "It's time to get to work. Iris, you already know where to go. Jake, let's go ahead and get you changed."

Iris stands from the table and makes her way up a small stairwell in the distance and into a control room type area overlooking the entirety of the building. Jake follows Caster out of the main area and into a back room lined with costumes.

"You have one hell of a set-up, Cas. I'm amazed that you've done all this in a matter of four years."

Smiling while running his hand along the costumes lining the racks, "When you have big supporters like I do, you tend to get whatever you ask for."

He reaches in and plucks a pair of tattered trousers from the rack and hands them to Jake.

"You will be playing a mindless, and shirtless barbarian type character that's going to be running around literally beating people up. Pretty easy gig, right?"

"Shirtless?"

Looking puzzled, Caster says, "Is that a problem? You told me you'd still been training, so I figured you would be in decent shape."

Lying, Jake says, "Uhm, ya man, it's no problem. I was just thinking of the mosquitoes in the jungle."

"Psh no worries, we're going to put so much makeup and oil on you, it'll be like trying to bite through a sheet of steel for them," mimicking rubbing oil all over himself.

He throws a pair of black boots over to Jake while snickering, "Go ahead and get dressed. It shouldn't take you too long."

Jake strips down as Caster stands around waiting and within a few quick movements, he dawns the costume. Caster looks him over to ensure the fit and says, "Looks good. Makes you look like a real killer Jakey boy."

"But I'm not a killer Cas," he quickly argues.

"Oh man, I'm sorry. I forgot." Caster places a hand on his forehead as if pretending to be in pain.

Changing the subject, he says, "I won't speak about it anymore. Let's go ahead and meet the team you will be *fighting* in the jungle."

Taking a deep breath to relax his building nerves, Jake follows Caster out of the main building and into the wilderness. Upon exiting the building, he can see a tough looking team of foreign troops standing by. He leans over to Caster and whispers, "These guys don't look like Panamanians."

Letting out a small chuckle, Caster says, "No Jake. Sadly, the Panamanian soldiers aren't exactly the best for the job. They're good for scaring away locals but not for precise tactical movements. I like my films to feel as authentic as possible."

"Got it."

Caster places one hand on Jake's back and pushes him toward the team, and exclaims, "Alright everybody! This is Jakey boy! He's pretty much going to run around the designated areas of the jungle, and you lot are going to beat each other up!"

A tough looking woman in all green camouflage tactical gear steps forward with her prop rifle and asks, "Where the hell is his shirt?"

"Dramatic effect my dear. He's a shirtless wild man that's going to *Kill* a few of you before getting captured and inevitably tortured to death. Sounds good to you?"

Wearing a face of disgust as she inspects Jake's form, she shrugs her shoulders and says, "Whatever you say boss. I'm here for the paycheck."

"Good. Now Jake," he turns to face Jake with hands on each of his shoulders, "It is very important that you follow their lead. Those are real rifles, and they will be shooting live rounds into the air and at the trees above you."

Widening his eyes and stepping back, Jake says with alarm, "Yo Cas! You never said anything about live weapons being pointed at me!"

Moving his hands to his hips, and shaking his head, Caster says, "Well Jake. Now you know why I film in Panama and not the U.S. There are much looser regulations when you have their Army commanders sleeping in the same camp as you. No worries though. As you can tell, I brought in American contractors to play the parts that require real expertise. You're in the best hands I can afford brother."

With his heart still pounding, Jake looks upon Caster's disappointed face, and allows his guilt to take over.

"Alright bro. But I-I want another thousand when all is said and done."

Caster looks up and places a finger to his chin like he is thinking and pauses for dramatic effect before saying, "Deal! Now go get em tiger."

The tough looking woman steps forward once again and jokingly says, "Let's go Tiger," and throws Caster a wink.

Raising a shaky thumb to his friend. Jake walks with the tough team of mercenaries into the dense jungle.

Hours of gun fire and screams fill the air, and as the sun begins to drop, the team returns from a gruesome day of fighting.

Caster stands by the main building and awaits their return. He leans against the side of the building, and sips on a crystalline cup of iced whiskey, and talks to a large man in an olive-colored uniform riddled with decorative ribbons. As Jake emerges from the jungle ahead of the team, he notices that the two men seem to be arguing. Quickening his pace and closing the distance between them, Jake shouts out, "Hey Cas! That was totally bad-ass bro!"

The angry uniformed man turns to look at the shirtless Jake through furrowed brow and a thick mustache before turning back to Caster and mumbling one last angry comment. He stomps his way into the building and Caster continues to sip at his whiskey with a carefree attitude.

"You good man? What was his issue?"

Pushing himself from the wall, Caster raises his glass to Jake and says, "No worry's bro. He just wants me to get to the climactic parts of the film. I told him you can't rush art, and he got mad. That is above your pay grade though. For now, why don't you go clean up and get some sleep. You have another early day coming up."

Looking at Caster suspiciously, Jake agrees and says, "No need to convince me. I'm about to crash right here. That team was tough on me. Some of them actually punched me in the face."

He rubs the left side of his face and laughs, "That chick has one hell of a right hook."

Looking at the purple swelling on Jake's face, Caster says, "She came highly recommended from a friend in the states. Cassandra is as tough as it gets."

Waving his hands about, he says, "I'll take your word for it. I'm going to get ready for bed. Is my mama in the tent already?"

Giggling obnoxiously now, Caster manages to say between laughs, "Bro she has been snoring for the past few hours. She even scared some soldiers standing guard."

Jake places a hand on his forehead. "Ya that sounds like her. Take it easy bro, I'll see you tomorrow."

The pair pound fists and part ways. As Jake turns his back and walks to his tent, Caster's high energy attitude fades and a serious look washes over him while he takes one last sip of his whiskey.

Heart to Heart

 *Like a wet blanket wrapping around his face, Jake runs through the thick humidity of the Panamanian Jungle with terror clawing at his heart, and echoing screams chasing him from afar. He clutches at his chest and feels a gaping hole beneath his breast. Letting out a deafening scream as he continues to run blindly through the night, a loud mocking laugh ripples through the air, and Jake cups his hands over his ears. Desperate to avoid the closing darkness, he looks beyond the nearing tree line, and sees a faint light in the distance. Running without rest, he wobbles, trips, and stumbles his way to the dim light and finally comes across a great oak door with a singular horned sconce attached to its frame. Without hesitation, Jake pushes the great door open and falls through the threshold as black smoke billows out at ground level. He looks up from the cold floor, and peers into the wood line behind, and sees darting shadows in the faint moonlight. Using his feet, he pushes the great door closed and the mocking laughter falls silent.*

He takes a deep breath as he struggles to his feet. Still feeling weak, he places one hand over the hole in his chest, and looks around in astonishment. Scared, yet amazed at what lay before him, he takes a few staggering steps and allows his

mouth to hang agape. He now stands in the middle of a round room lined in small white tiles and pure white grout with an assortment of colorful jewels neatly interwoven. Four entryways now lay before him, and yet only one is opened.

Untrusting of the open door, he stumbles to the first and pushes with all his might. Locked, with no door handle in sight, he tries the next. To no avail, he moves to the third. Yet again he finds himself helpless and staring at the fourth. He looks back toward the entrance he fell through and sees nothing but an empty white wall lined with the same taunting tiles and jewels. Having no other choice, he progresses to the fourth and final door. To his surprise, a man dressed in an all-black butcher's garb, wearing a white chef's apron and black nylon gloves, cuts at a lump of flesh laying on an old wooden table. Terror once again grasps Jake, but he cannot find the will power to step back. Rather, he is compelled to step forward. With his feet dragging him towards the figure before him, he tries to fight and starts to look around for a way out. What he sees instead only pushes his adrenaline to the max. Bodies tied to torture racks, entrails emptied on the floor, skin hanging from rotting arms and legs. Even stranger though, he notices that each body has been transformed and changed. Each corpse has an animal head graphed on like some freak show zoo, with perfect stitches and neat lines of staples marrying the transitional pieces of flesh.

He rips his head left and right, trying to tear away from his entranced body. Jake looks on in horror as the figure stops slicing his prey and turns. Tears swell up in his eyes, and he

*attempts to scream but nothing happens as a dry sensation
smothers his vocal cords. Instead, he is drawn to the figure
and looks deep into its eyes. A piercing green stares into his
soul and in an instant Jake stops fighting. A feeling of comfort
and familiarity wash over him, and he lets his hands fall to his
side. The figure stares back, never breaking eye contact.
Seconds pass as the feeling of comfort increases and the figure
lifts his palm to Jake's face and within it, lies a still beating
heart. Jake reaches out and-"*

Explosions fill the air and Jake is awakened with a massive
rumble in his stomach. A now wide-eyed Iris lets out a loud ear-
piercing scream that scares Jake more than the explosions.
Boom, boom, boom, as more explosions can be heard in the
distance, accompanied by bloody screams of terror.

"Jake! What the hell is going on?!"

"I don't know Mama! I think they're filming that war movie
out there!"

Caster comes bursting through the tent entrance and Iris
screams once more. Caster puts his hands over his ears with a
pained look and shouts, "Iris please!"

"What is going on?!" She asks, while crouching behind her
bed.

Uncupping his ears, Caster explains, "Our time line for the
explosions was moved up by the local government and I ran in
here to tell you before it started, but I was a little too late."

"Those screams sound awful and so real," she gestures
outside of the tent.

"Well Iris, if they didn't sound convincing, we'd never sell the movie," he jokes.

He turns to Jake and looking at his drenched shirt says, "It'll be fine bro. No need to panic."

Noticing Caster staring at the waterfall on the front of his shirt, Jake lets out a fake chuckle and says, "All good here. We'll just tuck back into bed and try to ignore the horror outside."

Laughing in unison, Caster says, "Alright you two. Get your beauty sleep because tomorrow, Jake will die!"

An eerie silence fills the air between them as Jake and Iris glance over at each other in shock.

"Oh noooooo! What I meant was, tomorrow Jake's character will die. If all goes well, you guys will be paid and, on your way, back into town and on a flight home within the week."

Pausing to let the situation defuse, he continues, "Unless you all want to stay until filming is done?"

Getting up from her crouched position and laying back in bed, Iris says, "No sir, no thank you, have a great night," and rolls over.

Jake shrugs his shoulders and waves goodnight as he too tucks himself back into bed while Caster makes his way out of the tent.

"*Damn, never thought I'd be happy to go back to NYC with Mama.*"

The dawn of a new day breaks the terror of the night. Jake sits straight up from his bed with bloodshot eyes and massive bags. Not able to catch another wink of sleep, he turns to his mother and can hear her snoring.

"If she snored any louder, I'd have to worry about earthquakes too!"

He throws his feet over the edge of the bed and begins to get dressed in his camouflage costume. Deciding he didn't want to walk around shirtless again, he throws on a thin gray hoodie and makes his way out of the tent. No longer surprised that Caster is up and about. Jake waves to him from afar. Caster pats a soldier on the shoulder and makes his way over to Jake from the main building's entrance.

"Damn brother. Do you ever sleep?" Jake asks.

"Sure, I do. It's all about the power naps my man."

They both laugh and Jake removes his right hand from his jacket, and gives Caster a half-ass salute while gesturing to the soldier.

"You know how it is bro. When you make the bigwigs money and entertain them, you also get the benefits of bossing their troops around. I can't say this job doesn't have its perks."

Looking around and admiring the hustle and bustle of everybody in the camp, Jake turns to Caster and says, "I wouldn't mind some of that authority back home. People are always running around like they are racing each other to the finish line."

Tilting his head in confusion, Caster says, "Finish line?"

"Ya bro. Death."

58

Smiling from ear to ear, Caster wraps one arm around Jake's shoulder and says, "Well we never know when we're going to die, now do we?"

Jake rolls his eyes at Caster and wittingly says, "Well according to you, I'm going to die today."

"Alright smart ass, let's get you situated with the team again and the day's suspenseful action will commence."

On the Run

 The sun's rays beam down, and Jake wipes sweat beads from his brow as he listens to the team leader, Cassandra, giving the mornings debrief.

"Listen up team. Today is going to be one of our main events. We have multiple more scenes to shoot in the coming month. Our newest team member Jake, is coming down to his final day on the set."

She turns towards him and beckons for him to step forward. He does as she instructs and finds himself standing in the center of the circular formation of iron skinned mercenaries. Peering around with a nervous look, he says through a toothy smile, "Caster told me that today is the day my character is supposed to die. Do any of you know how? It seems he may have changed some of the scenes for my *Death*."

A tall man with a clean shaved face, and a look to kill, leans against one of the beat-up jeeps nearby, and shouts, "Sure we do, pretty boy! Instead of skinning you, we're going to hang you after we catch your traitorous ass!"

Cassandra shoots him a look filled with daggers and the man clears his throat before rephrasing, "I mean, we're going to chase you about the jungle for a while, letting you beat us up, and then we'll get your final scene under wraps with an emotion felt hanging."

Jake's body stiffens as the rephrasing of their intent bounces through his skull, and he says, "You're going to lynch my character? Isn't that in poor taste?"

Cassandra places a hand on his shoulder and reassures him, "It's only racist if you make it that way. Everyone here is just excited to watch you in action, big guy."

His lungs begin to tighten, and breathing becomes a task. The sudden beads of sweat on his brow now become a downpour, and he says, "Can I speak to Cas before we get started?"

"Sorry big fellow, he's already on another shoot. We have clear instructions to get you geared up and to start the day. No worries though. I hear that your mother is going to be watching you through the cameras we have set up. I'm sure she'll be proud of you."

She snaps her fingers at a merc nearby, and he pulls a leather belt from the jeep and tosses it to Jake. He inspects the belt and within it is a small but very sharp knife. Noticing him staring at the small carbon blade, Cassandra leans her small frame towards him and says,

"Makes for a more realistic movie if the blade is legit. Just try not to stab yourself before the death scene."

Shakily he replies, "Uhm, alright."

Cassandra puts her hands to her mouth and whistles while gesturing for her team to get moving with a small circular motion above her head. Effectively and efficiently, the mercs load up their gear and mount the vehicles. Jake still stands clueless and afraid and looks to Cassandra for guidance. Before she can turn to look at him, the clean shaved man grabs Jake by the shoulder and says,

"You're with me, fella."

The wide-eyed Jake climbs into the rear passenger seat of the man's jeep and for the next hour, the team drives further into the jungle. They come to a slippery halt as the mud beneath the tires flings about. Everyone dismounts the vehicles and begins to line up near Cassandra's jeep.

"Jake!" she calls out.

"Yes Ma'am? He timidly yells from the rear.

"Just like the past few exercises, we're going to stage a scene with you in front of the tree cams. Do not pull that blade I gave you out unless I authorize it. Do you understand me?"

Moving his hands further from the blade as if it were a loaded pistol, Jake shakes his head in agreement.

Her face turns to stone as all expression fades away, and she yells, "Get into positions!"

Without hesitation, they break up into separate teams and begin sparring, and engage in tactical movements Jake has never seen in any movie before.

Once again, the shaved man sneaks behind him, and places a hand on his shoulder. Pulling Jake towards an area separate from the others, he whispers, "Time for some real action."

Unsure he can argue, Jake complies with this large man's aggressive guidance. He soon finds himself face to face with this overgrown baboon under a large tree with multiple cameras attached high in the air.

"Pull your blade, fella," he taunts. "I know you want to. From what I hear, you're a killer."

Cupping his hands together in front of his body, Jake says, "No not really. Cassandra said not to pull the knife without her approval."

"The hell with that little bitch! Pull your blade before I pull out mine!"

Staring into this behemoth's murderous eyes, Jake's hands tremble as he unsnaps the button holding the knife in place and raises it to chest level.

"Good, now try to stab me, fella."

The shaved man waves his hand invitingly while crouching forward a bit. Jake frantically looks around for help but doesn't see anyone to call.

"Where the hell is everyone! Cassandra help me!"

"Do it!" the man ravenously calls.

"No," Jake cries out, letting the knife drop to the ground with a soft thud.

"No?" The man repeats as he steps forward.

Like a flash of light, the shaven man chops Jake in the throat, and then shoulder tosses him to the ground like a rag doll. Clawing at his own throat and gagging, desperate for air, Jake panics and pushes himself backward with his feet. The man bends down and grabs the small knife, admiring its sheen. He looks to Jake still flailing on the ground, and smirks while waving the knife at him. Taking a large step forward, he kneels down on Jake's inner thigh.

Laughingly he says, "Time to see what your insides look like, fella!"

In one last desperate attempt, Jake looks around for help and lets out a blood-curdling cry. The man laughs and just as he goes to plunge the small blade into Jake's abdomen, a shot rings through the air. The man screams in pain, falling to the side, and clutching the hand that was holding the blade. With Jake still sobbing on the floor and grasping at his throat, the man looks around, and sees Cassandra standing on an elevated patch of dirt with her rifle in the firing position. His eyes fill with fear as Jake scrambles to his feet and leans against a tree nearby, and Cassandra begins to approach. In a distressed attempt to convince her it wasn't his fault, he begins to protest with a deep, yet failing voice.

"Ma'am he attacked me! I didn't know what else to do, so I threw him on the ground, and disarmed him! I think he wanted to stab me!"

Bypassing the cowardly shaven man, Cassandra walks over to Jake, and places a hand on his shoulder, "It'll be alright my friend."

Allowing her facial expression to stiffen with cruelty, she turns from Jake and faces the shaven man, while declaring, "I told you, we needed him alive for the final scene."

"Ma'am, I swear it wasn't my fault. What else was I supposed to do?"

Pausing, she takes a deep breath, and replies, "I believe you."

She walks over to the man's side, turning herself to face Jake, and gives him a friendly smile as she raises her rifle to the man's temple, and pulls the trigger. His body hit the ground with a loud thump, but Jake doesn't hear a thing. His brain goes silent, all pain dissipates, and he stands frozen. Watching the man's body lay motionless and bloodied, he shifts his eyes to Cassandras, and sees pure joy. Looking around the wood, he sees her team standing off in the distance, watching their leader murder her own trooper in cold blood.

Still staring Jake down, she vocalizes, "Fly little birdie, fly," and fires a shot into the air.

Jumping at the sound of the shot, Jake is snapped out of his shock, and bolts into the tree line. Anguished, he tries to keep to his feet, but slides around the muddy jungle floor, continuously tripping over logs while pushing himself deeper into the thicket.

"*Oh my god! Oh my god! They're going to kill me! Cas, where are you?!*"

He runs for what seems like an eternity. Jumping over small creeks, climbing the steep terrain of the nearing mountains, and sweating profusely. Peering back from time to time to ensure the band of Mercs are nowhere to be found, he stops to gain his bearings. Leaning against a large tree, Jake pants hard and tries to catch his breath. He looks up, with his back against the trunk, and whispers, "Where do I go? What should I do? I need to tell Cas."

Interrupted before he can complain any further, he hears a branch snap in the distance. Immediately he turns, placing his chest against the tree, and peers out from around its dark bark. Slowly observing the thicket, he can see the silhouette of multiple men crouching in the distance. Trying to contain his heavy breathing, he places one hand over his mouth, and slowly steps back. Crouching low, he turns from the tree. To his surprise, Cassandra is standing over him, with her rifle in hand. Jake freezes in place as panic sets in.

She looks him up and down, and says, "You suck," just before bashing him in the face with the butt of her rifle.

He falls to the ground, and lands in the soft mud. She beckons her men forward, and commands them to tie him up and drag him off. Silently they step forth and hog tie Jake. Two men slip a long log underneath his bindings, and they lift him into the air.

"He's ready for transport ma'am," one of her Mercs says.

"Good. Take this boring piece of meat to the hole. I need to radio Command and let them know what's happened."

The men nod, and begin to make their way through the jungle with Jake in hand, and Cassandra lifts a small radio to her mouth, "Command, this is Foxtrot, over."

Static fills the air, and she says again, "Command, this is Foxtrot, over."

Just then, Caster comes over the line, "Go ahead Foxtrot."

"We have an issue with Black Bird."

"Issue?"

66

"Affirmative Command, Black Bird tried to fly the coop ahead of the deadline. We've initiated transfer, and have moved Black Bird to the cage."

With no hesitation and a steady voice, Caster says, "Roger that Foxtrot. Carry on. Command out."

Caster turns in his chair and looks to Iris. "See how natural acting is for Jake. He made all of that look so real."

"He sure did. I don't know where you find these people, but they are so realistic."

Caster smiles at Iris and pivots to face the monitors. His expression blank, he watches as two of the Mercs carry Jake past the cameras, and toward an area just beyond their scope.

"So, what happens next? "Iris asks.

"Nothing much. Jake will hang out with that team in a separate camp for a day or two before he films his final scene. After that, you guys are home free, and on your way to having fatter pockets."

"Speaking about fatter. What's a lady to do to get some lunch?"

Caster spins around, chuckling at Iris' forwardness. "I'll get you something to eat. In the meantime, why don't you go downstairs and poke around some of the sets."

"Ow goodie. I've been wanting to poke around the romance set for a while. I saw about a hundred bottles of perfume that I wanted to smell."

She stands from her chair and makes her way down the stairs. Caster watches her every step, and then snaps his fingers to one of the guards nearby.

"Go ahead and get her some food. It'll be the last meal she'll enjoy for a while."

The guard nods his head and says with a heavy accent, "Yes sir."

Once the guard has walked away, Caster spins to the monitors while interlacing his fingers. Cracking them and yawning, he leans back in his seat and places his feet on the desk before him.

"This is going to be fun."

Forged in Darkness

 Sitting in a mud filled hole fifteen feet below ground level, Jake stares through the makeshift gate above.

"*If I could just reach one of those wood slats, I could lift myself out of this damned hole! How could I be so stupid?! I should have known this was all fake! But, Cas, of all people. Why?*"

Peering over the edge at the half nude body of his once friend Jake, Caster shouts down, "You still alive, Jakey boy?!"

Immediately irritation takes over and Jake snaps, "What the fuck do you want?!"

"That's rude. Haven't I taken care of you so far?"

"Ow you tried to take care of me alright. I just don't understand why."

Pursing his lips, Caster lets out a loud sipping noise after taking a swig of his coffee.

"Ya I guess I can tell you why now. I figured I wouldn't have to because you'd already be dead," he shrugs.

"Man, fuck you! I don't even care anymore!"

"Oh, don't lie to me, Jakey boy. I know it's burning you up inside."

"Whatever man."

"Okay, well if you don't want to know about your sister," he said, lifting his foot from the wooden gate and stepping back.

Jake shoots straight up from his seated position and screams, "Wait! What about Imani?!"

With a maniacal smile, Caster places his foot on the gate once more, and stares down at Jake, "Well, what can I say bro? She was getting stale and I was really bored. Honestly, I never truly loved her, but damn she was so fine it hurt to look away. I used to tear it up every chance I got, but eventually even that got boring. All she ever wanted to do was talk, and talk, and talk some more."

Grasping clumps of dirt in his hands to keep himself calm, Jake quietly listens as Caster tauntingly continues.

"Anyway! One day I started thinking about what she would look like without that pretty face, and next thing I knew, it was all I could think about. I used to sit at your small ass dinner table, looking right into her eyes and envisioning her face laying on my plate. Shit used to make me so hard, right there at the table and everything. While your daddy was too busy talking about how great you'd be in the ring, I was imagining cutting up his baby girl."

He pauses to take another sip of his coffee and watches Jake's expression, "You're not making this fun for me. Usually, my captures are screaming for mercy, or shitting themselves as I monologue. To be honest though, you're the first one to get put in the hole because you managed to run."

Jake looks away from Cas and stares at the dirt wall he leans against.

"You're a sick fuck, but I need to know what happened before I die."

Frowning at Jake's lack of emotion, Caster continues, "Whatever. I used to follow you guys all the time. Waiting for my moment to strike. I even paid a nearby bum with some crack, that night you both went into the park."

"The Park," Jake whispers to himself.

"You guys made it so easy for me. Playing around like you had no cares in the world. All I had to do was wait for you to step foot in the wood line, and we attacked."

He lets out a loud laugh, "You should have seen the look on her face when she saw that it was me. The sheer surprise and terror had my heart pumping so hard."

Unable to contain himself any longer, Jake shouts, "You motherfucker!" and throws clumps of dirt at the gate.

Stepping back to let the dirt fly by, Caster smiles and pours his scolding coffee into the hole.

"Ah fuck!" Jake screams in pain.

"Are you done, being rude? I haven't even gotten to the best part yet."

Ignoring Casters' never-ending taunts, Jake feels the weight of dread pulling him down, and sits in the corner of his prison, allowing the sun to shine in his face.

Noticing Jake fall silent, Caster clears his throat and calmly finishes his story.

"After we knocked you out, we gagged her, and dragged her out of the tree line. After that, Imani and I took a trip to your own neighborhood to have some fun. And Jake? The things we

71

did to her in the alley next to your apartment" he pauses to lick his finger as if licking a fine sauce with a loud smacking noise.

"I still find myself thinking about her to this very day. You never forget your first and well, I just had to have more," gesturing to the surrounding jungle.

"I gave the police my sob story and led them in the opposite direction of her body. It didn't take long for them to give up on finding another missing black girl from a shit hole area. The rest speaks for itself."

Looking at Cas with a burning hate in his eyes, Jake steadily asks, "Why did you bring me here?"

"You're a loose end my man, just like your daddy. After I spiked the bums' drugs and caused an overdose, I lurked around the streets and waited for your heartbroken father to start poking around the worst neighborhoods. He went down with one shot to his weak ass chest. He even called out my name and reached for my hand like I was supposed to help him."

Caster mockingly grabs his chest and cries out in pain.

"You guys fell apart with ease after that. But what I didn't expect was you, still out there looking for years. I knew I had to take action and lucky for me, it didn't take much to convince you to leave NYC. Honestly, I thought I'd have to bribe you more."

Feeling his adrenaline begin to redline, Jake stares at Caster with unwavering hatred, and lets out an earth-shattering primal scream. The veins on his forehead bulge, and steam writhes its way through the pores of his skin as the deep multi-toned reverberations rattle Caster's ears.

Caster smiles, and takes a step back in surprise. With energetic eyes, he peers back into the whole, and witnesses Jake still starting back. Bubbles of enjoyment begin to flow over, and Caster decides it is best to walk away before his many temptations take over.

"See you tomorrow bro," he says, stepping away from the hole.

The pounding of Jake's heart throbs throughout his head and the continuous drumming begins to drive him mad. Furiously, he punches at the dirt wall before him, and sends chucks flying everywhere. Clawing and punching until he can no longer stand. Jake falls to the muddy ground and lays motionless with eyes wide open.

Hours pass by, and yet he cannot compel himself to move. The night sky shines down into his prison, and Jake continues to stare into one of the dark corners across from him. His mind is blank and his soul lay bared, shattered into a million pieces. He begins to close his eyes in defeat, when a whisper reaches his ears.

"*Jake.*"

He snaps his eyes back open, and pulls himself from the mud. Looking up toward the gate, he expects to see a person. Nothing but empty sky and continuous moonlight reach his face. Puzzled, he sits back into a lit-up corner, and stares into the emptiness of his new home.

"*Jaaaaake.*"

His heartbeat spikes, and he closes his eyes. "Please go away. Leave me alone."

"*I will never leave you. We are one,*" The hushed voice claims.

He opens his eyes and in disbelief, he sees the silhouette of a man dressed in black crouching in the dark corner. Leaping up from the ground, Jake tears at the walls in desperation and tries to climb out. Glancing back to the corner, he now sees the man standing.

He yells, "Oh fuck!"

The whispering figure replies, "*Stop being ridiculous.*"

Unable to climb, Jake falls back to his corner and places his face to the dirt as he begins to say through faint sobs, "What do you want?"

"*I want what you want. We want vengeance.*"

Sniffling and wiping the dirt from his forehead, he turns toward the figure and questions, "Vengeance?"

"*Yes, Jake. Vengeance. For Imani. For Daddy. For all the innocents.*"

Hearing Caster's laughter rattle around his head, Jake says in dismay, "Daddy."

He and the figure pause, allowing time to elapse between them. Jake's heart begins to calm, and he stands tall.

"Come out of the shadows. Let me see you," Jake demands.

Seemingly floating forward, the figure becomes clearer and Jake's mouth falls agape. Looking directly at the figure, he sees himself, as if looking in a mirror.

"*As I said. We are one.*"

"I, I don't understand."

"Yes, you do. I've always been with you. Every Time you got mad. Every Time you got beat up in school and found the courage to fight back. When Imani was attacked, you raised your fists in defiance."

"But, what are you, and why are you following me?"

"We are one, now and forever. You weren't ready to see me yet."

"Ready?"

"Yes, Ready. You took the final step when you bloodied your hand saving that girl in glorious combat."

"Glorious combat? I'm losing my damn mind!"

Reaching out and touching the dirt wall, the figure says, *"No. You just needed to tap into your primordial side. Your true self. An energy as old as Earth, and as unwavering as the stars."*

Rubbing his temples and closing his eyes to think, Jake gets flashes of his dream and like a light bulb going off, knows the truth.

"It was you in my dream. You've been trying to tell me all along."

Finally, breaking the blank look upon his face. The figure allows himself to smile before saying, *"Every chill up your spine. Every gut feeling. Even smashing that security guard with Daddy's briefcase. All of it was me, or should I say, us."*

Jake looks to the floor and whispers, "Us."

"It's time Jake. Time to stand. Time to fight. Time to kill again."

"No! I can't kill again. I still hear the man from the park and the sound of his bones breaking."

"*All you must do is accept. Accept the fact that you are a savior of the innocent. Accept the fact that you, and few others have been able to unlock access to your true selves.*"

"Savior of the innocent? I'm a killer. I don't deserve to walk the world with the innocent."

"*Lies. What is more innocent than selfless love? Love for a stranger. Love for a mother. The unwavering ability to save and take a life in the name of something just.*"

Jake's heart beats steady, and all fear dissipates. He lifts his hands to the moonlight and observes them closely. No trembles, no fatigue, no doubt.

"I can feel you inside my head. I know what you say is true but I don't think I can do what you ask."

"*As I said, we are one. You just have to accept that fact and I will do the rest. In time, we will achieve pure harmony.*"

The figure raises a hand to Jake's face, and upon its palm lay a heart, beating, bleeding, and pure. Jake takes one hand from the moonlight and stretches it outward. He wraps his fingers around the heart, and makes eye contact with the figure. Green eyes pierce his soul, and two become one.

Alone in the Deep

The dawn of a new day breaks, and Caster be-bops his way to Jake's man-made prison in the ground. Holding a fresh mug of coffee, he whistles and smiles at the onlookers. Taking his time and avoiding the muddy puddles in his way, he stops to take a sip of his coffee and looks at the tree canopy above.

"I love the way the light barely breaks through the thicket. Such a pure and untouched environment."

Standing for twenty minutes or so to admire the jungle, Caster continues to deplete his mug. Letting out a loud smacking noise of satisfaction with his final sip, he exclaims with glee,

"Time to go see, Jakey boy!"

He trudges through the thicket and comes to the barren area around the hole. Cracking his neck in a circular motion, he prepares himself for the next part of his game.

"Ohhhhh, Jakey Boy!" he calls just before peering over the edge of the hole and placing his foot on the gate.

Unprepared for what he sees, he jumps back a step and shouts, "Yo!"

Jake hangs from a small tree root protruding from the dirt wall with one hand, not but four feet from the gate. With a blank stare, he pierces into Caster's soul.

"Get the fuck down, or I will shoot you here and now!" Caster yells, pulling his hand gun from the holster on his hip.

"What's the matter Cas? We thought you liked to play games."

"I said down!"

Not breaking eye contact, Jake lets go of the root and drops ten feet to the ground and lands without making a sound.

"Creepy motherfucker," Caster mumbles to himself before holstering his weapon.

He takes a deep breath and then assumes his taunting character's persona.

"Now that we've cleared up that creepy matter. I want to propose a new job to you."

Jake stares expressionless as Caster glares back with a puzzled look.

"Anyways, here's the deal. I have your mom convinced that this is all part of the movie we are making. Man is she dumb." he laughs.

"If you would like her to stay alive, you need to conclude our original agreement. You agreed to act for me and I'm feeling a little let down, Jakey."

Still staring Caster down, Jake cracks a maniacal smile and slightly lowers his head.

"Good, you're smiling. That means we have a deal. You get to run around the jungle tonight, and my men will hunt you down and kill you painfully. Sounds good?"

"Sounds good, Cas."

"You will get a one-hour head start when the sun goes down. If you die... when you die, I should say. Your mother will be returned to the states with a large chunk of cash. Free to live out the rest of her few years, thinking that you will be staying on to film a little longer."

"*He's Lying,*" *the voice whispers to Jake.*

Slightly nodding his head in acknowledgment to the voice, Caster takes it as an agreement.

"That's pretty much the gist of it. Do you have any questions?"

Jake slowly shakes his head no, while maintaining eye contact.

"See you at sundown!" Caster yells out, taking his foot from the gate and walking away with an irritated look.

"*He noticed our lack of fear. It will eat him alive,*" *the voice whisperingly says, followed by a maniacal chuckle.*

Standing motionless and unafraid, Jake stares up toward the gate and watches as the sun slowly makes its way over his prison and through the sky. Another humid night begins to creep closer and Jake smiles.

"*It's time.*"

"Yes, it's time," Jake agrees.

Bending his knees slightly, Jake pushes from the ground and propels himself upward. Reaching the gate and clinging on with one hand, he extends an arm outward and rips the lock off with a single yank. It only takes a moment before Jake finds himself free, and walking into the thicket of the coming night. Step after step, he descends into darkness. As silent as the wind, he progresses so far into the wood, the naked eye would be unable to see among the trees.

"This is far enough. Say the words."

He falls to his knees, chest still bare for all to see, shoeless, and fearless, he says collectedly, "We are one. Now and forever."

He closes his eyes and places his hand on his heart, "I relinquish control."

The wind whips through the jungle and the creaking of trees and rustling of leaves can be heard all around. He lowers his hand from his heart and opens his eyes. A radiant green peeks out from behind his lids, and a grimace of pleasure contorts his face.

Meanwhile, Caster stands in the control room, littered with monitors and asks, "Are you ready, Iris? Tonight, Jake's character is going to go out with a bang. He's been practicing the past few days out in the jungle with some of our crew. He told me to tell you that he couldn't wait for you to see the amazing effects."

"Oh lord, he always has been a dramatic one. Thank you again sweetheart."

Caster smiles at Iris, and kisses the back of her hand before turning to the door and exiting down the stairs. Whistling and feeling gleeful, Caster exits the large building and makes his way to Jake's prison. He pulls a small flashlight from the cargo pocket of his tactical pants and clicks it on. The jungle illuminates as if the sun itself has come back to play.

Caster gestures to a lone soldier standing guard and says, "Come on, I might need some help to get him out."

The soldier says something in Spanish and salutes as he follows Caster down the muddy path leading to hole in the ground. Taking their time, Caster lets out an obnoxious loud yawn and cracks his neck. A few minutes go by before they reach the open area around the prison, and Caster stops dead in his tracks.

"Why is the gate open?" he asks.

The soldier shrugs his shoulders and grabs for his radio. Caster snatches it from his hands and radios the control room.

"Command this is Caster; Black Bird is loose and in the jungle. Deploy the mercenaries."

Sitting in the control room with an excited look. Iris gazes at the screens with wonder and says, "You guys are so good. I can't wait to watch the movie when it's all put together."

The soldier sitting nearest to her smiles and gives her a nod before answering Caster.

With a heavy accent, he says, "Sir, the team has deployed and should be closing in on your location soon."

Caster throws the radio back to the soldier standing by and walks up to the hole. Maneuvering his flashlight over the edge, he peers inside.

"He must have been helped. There is not a rope, nor a ladder to be found."

81

Turning his gaze from the hole, he looks to the muddy ground and within seconds, finds what he is looking for. Crouching down, he plucks the broken lock from the mud and questioningly says, "It was broken, not cut? What the hell is going on?"

He throws the lock to the wayside and yells to the soldier, "Stay here and wait for the Mercs! Make it painful! I'll be watching from command," and hastily walks away.

The soldier throws half-hearted salute and proceeds to awkwardly stand in the deep thicket of the night.

Animals in a Zoo

Preparations are underway, and Iris is none the wiser as she sits in her chair gleefully watching Caster and his men freak out in the control room.

"*They are doing such a great job. My baby is going to be a superstar after this film.*"

"Pan to every camera we have in the vicinity and I want the footage for the last few hours playing on as many monitors as we can manage! Black Bird couldn't have gotten too far! Cease him and bring him back to the hole," Caster barks to every soldier within earshot.

"Black Bird sounds like some super hero name!" Iris cheerfully says.

Caster ignores her presence and continues to watch the screens for any sign of Jake. Feeling himself get more aggravated by the second, he pounds his fists on the desk.

"*I knew one of them would eventually escape. I never thought it would be Jake though. He's always been too weak for a good fight.*"

The door to the command center bursts open and everyone jumps as it smashes against the wall. Caster turns to look at the disturbance and sees the large uniformed man with multicolored ribbons staring him down.

With a heavy accent he says, "You lost the asset? You assured me this was going to be worth all the money we have invested in this operation."

"Captain, now is not the time. I have an old friend to kill."

"Then when is the time Mr. Roderick? I have seen you butcher countless people at this facility and yet you continue to bore me. You have until sunrise to find this idiot running around my jungle or else it will be you on the torture rack."

Caster stands wide-eyed and attempts to say, "No worries Cap-" but the Captain pivots on his heel and exits the door before he can finish.

Meanwhile, the giddy look on Iris' face has dissipated and worry takes its place.

"*An old friend to kill. Why would he say that?*"

She turns to the beet red Caster and asks, "Caster what did you mean by an old friend to kill? It didn't sound like it was scripted."

He removes his hands from the desk and with furry in his eyes, says, "That's because we've been lying this whole time Iris. I'm going to kill Jake, and then I'm going to peel your face from that sorry sack of bones you call a body."

Before Iris can respond or move, Caster takes a few steps towards her, unholsters his weapon, and bashes her over the head. Iris falls from the chair and lands on the floor with a loud thump.

"Take this useless flesh bag out of my sight. Tie her up and leave her in the maintenance closet."

Two soldiers salute and drag her away. Caster turns his attention to the monitors once more and continues his search for Jake.

Cassandra and her mercenary team finally reach the man-made prison, and she peers into the hole for clues. With no sign of assistance or climbing tools, she begins to wonder how he managed to escape. With two fingers, she signals for her team to slip up and take different sides of the tree line as she goes down the middle. With flashlights on blast, they progress twenty paces at a time before pausing, and observing the jungle for signs of movement. Cassandra looks down to the ground and sees a very wide spaced set of tracks. Snapping her fingers and signaling for her team to move in the direction of Jake's tracks, she lifts her rifle to the ready. Pushing forward, bit by bit. Cassandra feels her ego take hold.

"Come on out Tiger! We just want to play!"

Nothing but silence accepts her taunts, and she tries once more.

"Jakey, Jakey, Jakey! Come out, come out, wherever you are!"

The wind around her picks up and the rustling of the tree canopy above increases. The sound of bending branches and creaking trees fill the air. Cassandra yells at her team to keep an eye out, but no one can hear her. Breaking formation, she walks over to the nearest Merc and puts a hand on his shoulder. "I said, eyes up! This weather is going to make things harder!"

The Merc looks her in the eyes and nods his head. He turns and takes a step forward. Just then a shadow blazes by and the merc goes flying into the dark canopy above. Jumping back, Cassandra raises her rifle high into the air and suddenly the wind stops and the creaking of the trees dissipates. Screaming can be heard in the distance, high above the team. Everyone turns around and raises their weapons and flashlights high into the air.

"You see that, Cassandra?" A shaky Merc calls out.

"No shit I saw that. I was standing right there, idiot. Stay sharp, I need to radio Command."

She takes a knee in the mud and pulls out her radio, "Command this is Foxtrot, over."

Without hesitation, Caster comes over the line, "Report Foxtrot. Have you found Black Bird?"

"That's a negative Command. There's something else out here though. Something we didn't see."

Annoyed at their incompetence, Caster replies, "What do I pay you for? Just shoot the damn thing and then bring Black Bird back to me, now!"

"But sir! Whatever it is, it ripped one of my men up into the air! Listen!"

She holds down the key to the radio and outstretches her arm high into the dark sky. The screaming of her Merc continues, and he begins to make gurgling sounds as he chokes on blood.

"You hear that asshole? That's coming from up in the tree canopy! I don't know what sick games you're playing, but my team is not going to be part of it," she fearfully yells.

"I hear it, Foxtrot. That doesn't change the fact that you have a job to finish! Now get out there or I will send in the Captain's troops to hunt you both!"

"Fuck you and the Cap-" A loud crash and scream interrupt her sentence and Cassandra whips around to see one of her Merc standing lifeless, impaled by a large log protruding from the ground like some giant spear.

"Turning to her team, she yells, "Run!"

They do just that and all hell breaks loose. Taking the lead in guiding them back to the compound, Cassandra's mercenaries follow close behind. Through the splattering of mud under foot and the hurricane winds that have re-emerged, she can hear the defining screams of her men from behind.

"This is not how I die! Fuck this place! The legends are true, the Devil lives in this Jungle!"

Putting all her weight behind each step in an effort to propel herself forward, she loses her footing and slips in the mud. Falling backward while sliding, she witnesses a spear-like log wiz over her head with one of her men still attached. It makes contact with a nearby tree and gets logged inside its thick hide. Laying on her back, slipping about trying to get up from the mud, she stares at the disfigured body as blood pours forth from every crevice.

Finally managing to get to her feet, she drops her rifle and runs as fast as she can to the nearing lights of the compound ahead. Breathing heavier than she has in a long time, she feels a sense of relief wash over her as a soldier comes into sight. Noticing the winds die out, she allows her pace to slow. Peering back into the fading dark, she lets out a sigh of relief before turning back towards the lights of camp. As her face comes back around, a wild man with piercing green eyes stands before her. She collides with his body and falls backward. Like hitting a wall at full force, her forehead busts open, and blood gushes from the chasm in her skin. Raising a hand to her head and opening her eyes wide in an attempt to focus her blurry vision, she looks up to see Jake standing over her.

He cocks his head to the side and with a great smile on his face, says, "You suck!" and rips her off her feet. Cassandra lets out a blood-curdling scream of pure terror, and all the nearby guards turn from their posts and peer into the jungle. Only a few are unfortunate enough to see Cassandra ripped into the high canopy above by a fast shadowed mist with no form. Scrambling backward, they begin to shout, "The Devil is here! Run!"

Mania

Watching the monitors in disbelief, Caster looks upon the multitude of bodies hanging from trees, speared into the ground, and even puddles that no longer have form.

"What the fuck happened to the Mercs? Looks like an animal got to them."

A loud raid siren begins to blare outside, and Caster turns his attention to the camera monitors for the immediate compound. He sees troops running around in circles like they don't know which direction to go. Switching from monitor to monitor, he attempts to find the culprit of their distress but can't find one.

"What the hell are these idiots running from?"

Reaching over to a console full of buttons and switches, he turns a knob and increases the volume to one of the cameras. He listens carefully for noises but all he can hear is the men yelling, "It's the Devil! The Devil has come!"

Still panning back and forth between monitors, Caster becomes more confused by the second. Men jumping in vehicles and driving away, others standing post with rifles at the ready, and even some running towards the main facility.

"You and you, go get the Captain and find out what's happening! Lock the door on your way out! We don't need them bringing whatever it is inside!" he barks at his guards.

The guards scurry away and a look of worry washes over Caster.

"Maybe the townspeople are finally coming to stop us. No, the Captain would have dealt with that like he did before. What is it then?!"

Irritation and anticipation continue to rise as he watches the screens with his full attention. Turning to the monitor displaying the fleeing vehicles, he looks upon the taillights distancing themselves from the compound and within a blink of his eye, they disappear into the night sky. Standing from his chair in surprise, he leans towards the monitor and sweat begins to form on his upper lip. He reaches out and checks the connections to the screen but can't find any issues with the cabling.

"Tail Lights can't fly, and neither can cars! What the hell is going on!"

Screaming fills his ears and men begin to pound on the locked doors of the building. Turning to the closest entryway, he places one hand on his pistol. Taking a breath of relief as the door holds fast, he unsnaps his pistol and lays it on the table before him as a persuasion. Watching through the monitors, he can see men scratch and claw at the door while looking back in fear, his eyes bulge, and he dare not blink as spurts of blood fill the air.

Watching multitudes of troops scramble about with weapons at the ready and piss filling their pants, Jake continues to stand in the tree line of the dark jungle. An emotionless expression holds his face and with little effort, he transmutes into a shadow and makes his way to the only road leading from the compound. Vehicle engines roar to life as troops load up and try to flee. Standing in the middle of the muddy road, Jake waits for them to approach. Doing as he expected, they pull out of the parking area with high beams and weapons on high alert. A plethora of metal beasts descend upon him, and yet he dares not move. Instead, he raises his hands in a beckoning motion and with a simple upward swipe, the first of the vehicles flies into the night sky. Tail lights fade into the distance and a loud crunch of metal and flesh resonate throughout the air.

Spreading his legs and assuming a sumo squat, Jake pulls both arms back with hands at chest level and motions forward as if propelling the shadows themselves. The second of the vehicles crumples like a can and is thrown backward into the next. A loud explosion and flames fill the night and all others in the convoy come to a slippery stop. Watching the men flee from their vehicles and into the tree line, Jake stands straight and yet again, transmutes himself into a dark, shadow filled smoke. Men shout and their bloody screams can be heard all around the jungle as Jake swiftly kills each of them, one by one.

Standing post with shaky hands and darting eyes, the remainder of the troops listen to the distant explosions and screams bouncing around the jungle. Illuminated vehicles burn in the distance and fear creeps into their hearts.

One man steps out of the line that has formed in front of the main building's locked doors. Creeping his way forward while looking side to side for any sign of life, he mutters, "Looks all clear guys."

Turning from the jungle and looking to his peers, he begins to make eye contact when all of a sudden, he lets out a bloody gurgling sound, and is raised into the air as his spine contorts backward. The mouths of the remaining men fall agape as Jake stands behind the whining soldier with his hand wrapped around the blooded interior of his spine. He turns his radiant green gaze from the man in his hand, and peers at the line of troops.

One man, without a rank on his uniform, yells, "Fire!"

A barrage of bullets careen towards Jake, and he dissipates into black smoke and reappears to their right. With one swipe of his hand, he cuts a soldier in half, sending blood and guts spurting on the wall and the others. Transmuting again, he reappears on their left as they still shoot to the right. He reaches through a soldier and rips his heart out backward, leaving a hole with connective tissue oozing fluids.

With a series of transmutations, Jake makes quick work of the others and leaves a mess of blood and limbs splattered across the building entrance and the surrounding walls. He walks to the door with confident strides, and stops to look up at the camera. Tilting his head with a deadpan expression, he evaporates into a cloud of black smoke.

Casters guards come bolting through the side door of the building with the Captain in tow. Lacking any hesitation, they make their way up the stairs and into his presence.

"Sir the Captain is here!" One shouts.

Remaining motionless with eyes fixated on the monitors, Caster utters, "He disappeared like some fucking ghost."

With his khaki-colored uniform drenched in blood, the Captain puts a hand on Caster's shoulder and rips him around.

"What the fuck are you doing?! All of my men outside are dead because of you!"

Staring at the Captain, Caster smoothly reaches for his pistol on the table and then fires four shots into his chest.

In a casual tone, Caster says, "I told you not to touch me."

Turning his focus to the two soldiers staring at the lifeless body of their Captain, he says, "One of you go get Iris, I think it's time we use our bargaining chip against our friend and you, go get me my special box."

Too fearful to move suddenly, they skip the salutes and formality to creep out of the command center.

"Alright Jakey, where did you go?"

He pans through the monitors looking for any sign of movement, but instead sees the grounds of the compound littered with body parts and blood. He cracks his neck with both hands and takes a deep breath to steady his heart.

"It's show time."

Hearing the distant footsteps of his soldiers approaching, Caster turns toward the stairs and sees Iris bound and gagged. He motions for her gag to be removed and turns to the soldier with the box.

"Go put the box on the table downstairs by the main entrance. I want him to open my gracious surprise."

Without a word, the soldier makes his way downstairs and carries out the command. Meanwhile, the other soldier ungags Iris and pushes her towards Caster.

"Go ahead and take a seat Iris. We are going to wait for Jake to enter the building, and then we're going to have some fun."

Lifting his pistol to the soldier he says, "Now get down stairs and defend the door with your friend."

Running off in fear, the soldier makes his way down the stairs and to the front door. Unable to control the trembles throughout their bodies, each soldier unholsters their pistols and points at the entrance with shaky aim.

From up above, Caster spins Iris' chair toward the giant window overlooking the main entrance, and puts his pistol to her head.

"Any minute now. Jake must know we have you. He's already killed everyone else."

Wide-eyed she exclaims, "No, my baby wouldn't hurt a fly unless he had too! He's not a killer like you!"

Caster bumps Iris in the temple with his pistol and says, "That's right, I am a killer. You'd do well to remember that. I won't go as easy on you as I did your weak ass hus-"

The doors to the main entrance burst open and a black smoke pours forth. The soldiers shoot wildly, hoping to kill whatever slithers before them. Unsuccessful in their endeavor, they both make a brief gagging noise before landing on the ground, dead.

Materializing before their eyes, Jake stands shirtless, shoeless, and wearing tattered camouflage trousers. Just as Caster had left him.

Ensuring Jake can hear him, Caster begins to shout, "Hey Jakey boy. Glad you could join us. I left a present on the table for you. Why don't you go ahead and open that box? It's what you came here looking for after all."

Looking up to the window of the Command center, Jake's blazing green eyes petrify Caster where he stands.

Iris, noticing his eyes, says with worry, "That's not my Jake anymore, I don't know who that is."

Turning his gaze from above, he looks to the box on the table, and reaches out with one hand to remove the lid. Standing expressionless, he plunges an open palm into the box and pulls out the head of a mannequin. Sown upon its white lifeless frame is the weathered and crumbling face of his sister, Imani.

Able to move once again, Caster tauntingly yells to Jake, "It's unfortunate, but she's in a poor state. I hadn't perfected my craft yet," gesturing to the surrounding facility."

Watching Jake staring at the leathery face of his sister, Caster presses the pistol hard against Iris' face and shouts, "Time to say goodbye to mommy!"

95

However, before he can get a chance to pull the trigger, Jake evaporates and materializes behind him. Not having enough time to turn and react, Caster's face shifts to fear as Jake wraps both hands around his head, and rips it from his body.

Blood sprays over the back of Iris and she screams. Leaping from the chair, she moves away from the fallen body and darts behind her son. A few moments pass as she watches Jake twitch from behind as he holds Caster's head.

"Jake, baby? What are you doing?"

Unresponsive, he continues to move his hands about Caster's head and his own. She outstretches a faltering hand and places it against his shoulder. He stops moving, and stiffens.

With a quivering voice, she asks, "Jake?"

Dropping Casters' bloodied head to the floor, he turns to Iris in an apathetic state. She releases her grip and throws herself back, tripping and landing on the ground. Standing above her, he cocks his head and with his hellish green eyes, peers through the fleshy skin of Casters face placed over his own, while saying in a hushed tone,

"Jake? No Jake here. We are the Harbinger of their destruction."

Coming in 2021:

Cry of a Valkyrie

By
C. M. Schrecengost

About the Author

C. M. Schrecengost is a Marine Corps veteran who loves the beach bum life of North Carolina, and soaks up the sun, while listening to the waves with his wife and daughters.